4

FICTION

NON-FICTION

Neil Clarke: Publisher/Editor-in-Chief
Sean Wallace: Editor
Kate Baker: Non-Fiction Editor/Podcast Director
Gardner Dozois: Reprint Editor

Clarkesworld Magazine (ISSN: 1937-7843) • Issue 94 • July 2014

© Clarkesworld Magazine, 2014
www.clarkesworldmagazine.com

The Contemporary Foxwife
YOON HA LEE

Kanseun Ong was procrastinating on her end-of-term assignment by puzzling over a letter from her older father when the doorbell chimed. At first she didn't react, even though correspondence from home—specifically from Older Father—was the last thing she wanted to deal with. Older Father was only fluent in their ancestral language, Na-ahn, which Kanseun spoke shakily and hardly read at all, and was a calligrapher as well; he liked to show off by sending her paper letters. He wrote every four weeks, if the dates were to be believed, although due to the vagaries of ship traffic the letters arrived more irregularly. The letters piled up in a box, the early ones forever unopened, and Kanseun felt both guilty and resentful on a regular basis. Her entire childhood her fathers had told her how important it was for her to perfect her Kestran, the unofficial official language of the Sasreth Alliance, so why subject her to this now that she was a student at Veroth station? Especially since Older Father knew she was only ever going to write back in Kestran?

The doorbell chimed again, more loudly. She'd programmed it to do that precisely because it irritated her. "Who is it?" she asked crossly.

"No one is present at the door," the apartment's watcher said in a distinctly bored voice. Had her roommate been messing with its personae again? Osthen-of-*White Falcon*, who would also be her best friend if only they would ever tidy up after themselves.

"No, really," Kanseun said. Hadn't she already had the talk with Osthen about how she needed quiet time this week to work on the concerto she had due? Not that she was working on it right now, but that was a detail. She should have known that Osthen had agreed too quickly, even if she'd all but agreed to pay them to meet up with their many loud friends elsewhere.

1

"No one is present at the door," the watcher repeated, still bored.

Kanseun cursed and put the letter down, tucking it under a paperweight in the shape of a disgruntled turtle. (Her younger father had a thing for turtles.) "Show me what's in front of the door," she said. A prank? She might not be an engineering candidate like Osthen, but she was good at jiggering security, and anyone messing with her was in for a nasty surprise.

The monitor displayed nothing but—was that a flicker? A curlicue of shadows?

She got up and opened the door just to check. *If Osthen's fucking with me on another stupid dare,* she thought, *I'm going to throttle them. "No one is present at the door" my ass.*

"Hello! Very pleased to make your acquaintance," said the no-one-is-present-at-the-door. It looked and sounded remarkably like a gawky teenage boy with tawny skin, black hair falling past his shoulders. Spectacles garnished with little amber-colored crystals framed large, long-lashed eyes. Who on earth needed spectacles anymore? Unless it was a fashion trend elsewhere in the station. His russet dress, or gown, or whatever it was, looked like it had led a former life as a sack, except the sleeves had hems. For all that, the boy smelled sweetly of clover and damp grass and disintegrating pine needles. Plants that were in short supply on the station, although Kanseun was planetborn and recognized the scents.

The bespectacled no-one-is-present-at-the-door, undeterred by what Kanseun had hoped was her most forbidding expression, was still speaking: "Are you in need of a foxwife? I cook, do dishes, scrub floors"—who did any of that except as a hobby?—"arrange flowers, disarm bombs, perform minor surgery, and provide comfort and companionship." She?—they?—radiated hopefulness at Kanseun.

"You're a what?" Kanseun said intelligently, using Kestran's alt form of the second person pronoun, acceptable either for actual alts, like her roommate, or when you had no clue whatsoever.

"I'm a boy foxwife," the foxwife said helpfully.

"Sorry," Kanseun said, chastened. Even if nothing in her previous experiences had prepared her for any type of foxwife.

"It's all right," he said, and dimpled at her.

It registered that he had said "foxwife" not in Kestran, but in Na-ahn. Kanseun remembered the word only because she had loved the animal spirit stories Older Father had told her as a child, in the early days before she went to school and lost the ability to say anything but *Pass the sauce, please* and *How's the weather?* "Foxwife" rendered straightforwardly as "fox" plus "wife." In all other regards, the foxwife was speaking a very polite form of Kestran. Too polite; it wasn't as though an unproven artisan candidate merited it.

Why did this matter? The boy was clearly cracked. "Listen," she said, trying not to talk down to him, "if you need Transient Services, they're not on the university level, they're on Level 18. You can get directions at any of the info kiosks."

The foxwife had peered around her into the room and was eyeing Osthen's couch—more accurately, the food wrappers on the couch—with interest. Was he hungry? "I can also tidy things and file papers and dust under couches," he said.

"Hey," Kanseun said, "the messy half of the room is *not* mine." Too late she realized she was encouraging him, and she steeled herself to be more firm.

To her surprise, the foxwife drooped and said. "All right. Thank you for your time. I hope you lead a long life with many blessings!"

What? "Hey, wait," Kanseun said. She was going to regret this, but she was noticing the smudges under his eyes, imperfectly concealed by cosmetics. Asking how long he'd been a transient—if, indeed, that was what he was—would be rude. Instead, she said, "Look, I'm not supposed to randomly take in more roommates, but why don't you come in and have some tea, and we'll figure out what to do." At least Osthen wouldn't mind; they were friendly to a fault.

She was getting more creative at procrastination, no doubt about it.

"I brew tea, too," the foxwife said, brightening.

"Oh no you don't," Kanseun said. She wasn't *that* much of a grouch. "You're my guest. I'm providing the tea." Where did he come from that people brewed their own tea or did the dishes? Was he one of those weird people who believed that tea perfection could only be achieved that way?

For that matter, *filing papers*? Too bad she couldn't have him answer her letters for her, but that would be tacky. Maybe tomorrow she'd procrastinate some more by scribbling the usual vague persiflage about how well she was getting on with her roommate (more or less true), complaining about the everyday sameness of station weather (always good for a few sentences), and how hard she was working at her music studies (true except when he sent her letters).

The apartment's watcher had picked up on her offer of tea. Two fragrant cups awaited her on a tray in the kitchen. She wasn't entirely sanguine about leaving the foxwife alone in the living room, but she didn't think he was dangerous, just a little out of touch with reality.

Kanseun emerged with the tray only to find the foxwife on his hands and knees, diligently picking up Osthen's collection of hand-painted tradeship figurines and organizing them on the nearest available table. She gaped, then said, "You don't need to *do* that. That's my roommate's mess. It's *their* problem."

"Oh, but I want to be useful!" the foxwife said.

Kanseun suppressed a sigh as she set the tray down. "Were you going door to door offering your, er, services for a long time?"

"Yes," he said without elaborating.

How had he escaped having *really bad things* happen to him, wandering around like this? To say nothing of this being the most inefficient job-seeking method ever. "How many people did you talk to?"

The foxwife frowned and brought up one hand, then the other. Kanseun realized he was counting on his fingers. When he got to ten he stopped and tilted his head. "Lots?" he said. "More than two paws, anyway."

Paws. Right. She was in over her head, but she'd promised tea. "Paws" wasn't that much stranger than some of the slang going around the university anyway. "Here," she said. "Sit down." She indicated her side of the room, which included a chair that wasn't obscured by a pile of game controllers. "What do I call you? I'm Kanseun Ong."

He sipped the tea delicately. "I'm a foxwife," he said with disarming happiness.

"Are you Norannin?" she asked. "You seem to speak a little of my ancestral language."

"I don't know," he said. "I speak a little of everything! I like languages."

So much for that. "Where do you come from?" She was being terribly direct considering they'd just met, but as long as he didn't mind—

The foxwife considered the question. "I walked a lot," he said finally. "I think I took some wrong turns, though."

Walked? To a space station? Granted, Veroth wasn't without its shabby underworld, but she couldn't believe that someone wouldn't have scooped up the foxwife before long. Transient Services prided itself on its thoroughness. "How long have you been on the station?"

By now the foxwife's cup was half-empty. One of the watcher's puppets came out to fill it up again. "Thank you," the foxwife said, still politely.

"You're welcome," the watcher's voice said warmly.

Kanseun blinked.

The foxwife sipped. "I got here"—the fingers again—"four days ago."

Kanseun didn't memorize the roster of ships incoming and outbound, but it was impossible to escape hearing about them. Like many ship-clanners, Osthen couldn't imagine *not* knowing these things. Thanks to Osthen, Kanseun knew that the only ship that had made port four days ago was the battle cruiser *Marrow*. Despite Osthen's jokes about warclanners, she doubted that they would be so lax as to have allowed the foxwife to stow away.

She decided that the mystery was going to be someone else's problem, and drained her cup in one long gulp. The watcher had given her lukewarm tea, overly sweetened, her preference.

"Osthen is at the door," the watcher said. It had returned to boredom.

"Wonderful," Kanseun said just as the door swooshed open and Osthen slouched through it. Today their hair was done up in looped braids tinted purple at the ends. "Osthen—"

She looked around. Where had the foxwife gone?

"Hey there," Osthen said. "You missed a great party, by the way. Anyone call for me?"

"No, but—"

Interesting. There was a new table in the corner, polished red-black, exquisite in its sleekness. Kanseun had never seen it before. She tried not to be alarmed.

"Hang on," she said to Osthen, who looked bemused. "You can come out now," she called to the foxwife. "My roommate's a slob, but they won't hurt you. Their name is Osthen-of-*White Falcon*."

Before Osthen had time to ask why she was addressing a *table*, the foxwife was sitting cross-legged on the floor where the table had been. He bounced to his feet and said, "Hello! I'm Kanseun's new foxwife." This time he rendered the word in Kestran. He bobbed a bow to Osthen.

Osthen grinned at Kanseun. "I knew you'd get laid sooner or later."

"*Excuse* me," Kanseun said, queasy on the foxwife's behalf. Among other things, she wasn't convinced that he understood the connotations of "wife." And had Osthen really not noticed the transformation? "Do I look like I've just gotten laid?" Osthen opened their mouth and she hurried on. "He's, uh, visiting until I can help him get settled."

"Hello, foxwife," Osthen said, their grin softening into a more genuine smile. "Stay as long as you need to, that's what the couch is for. And don't mind Kanseun, she's always got a stick up her—"

"Oh, shut up," Kanseun said.

"Anyway," Osthen said without breaking stride, "I need to catch up on sleep. Later." They drifted past her and the foxwife in a haze of musky perfume and into their room. A moment later the door shut definitely.

If only she, too, had the ability to fuck around all the time and still get perfect scores on everything. "Could you explain what is going on here?" she said to the foxwife, remembering the watcher's *No one is present at the door* with ice-splash clarity.

"I'm very good at furniture," the foxwife said. "Did you like it? I do vases, too, but I didn't think it would harmonize with your design sense. My sister, now—my sister would have come up with a vase that worked. But I—" He stopped.

"It was a very nice table," Kanseun said, so that she didn't feel like she was kicking a child. She wanted to ask about the sister, but she sensed it was too early in their acquaintance. "Does this always happen around you? Why did I notice but Osthen didn't?"

The foxwife said, with the air of someone explaining the obvious, "I'm *your* foxwife." He picked up a broom from where it had been leaning against the wall, except Kanseun knew for a fact that there had been no broom there earlier, let alone one made of *straw*, and started sweeping.

"You don't have to *do* that," she said. "The watcher puppets that stuff."

"I like sweeping," the foxwife said placidly.

"Fine," Kanseun said. "I am officially not dealing with any more of this stuff tonight. I am going back to my nice, sane concerto and figuring out what the hell I have to do to balance my percussion line so I can cough up the rest of this movement. You do what makes you happy."

The foxwife's gaze became anxious. "Is it bothering you?"

"Yes. No. Oh, do what makes you happy. I guess it's no worse than meditation."

He resumed sweeping.

"Right," Kanseun said. She sat at her desk and stared at her score, willing it to cooperate.

She never did respond to the day's letter, nor the one after that, even though she could feel Older Father's disappointment radiating through the envelopes at her.

Facts about Kanseun's foxwife, if not all foxwives:

His favorite food was jam. It didn't matter what kind. Kanseun had expected him to eat something logically vulpine, such as eggs. He liked eggs too (any kind with runny yolks, including raw), but there was no denying how happy he looked when he sat on a stool in the kitchen and ate jam out of a little dish with a spoon. The first time she caught him eating it straight out of the jar, but fortunately he was amenable to changing his habits.

When he said he spoke a little of everything, he wasn't kidding. After Kanseun handed in her concerto—2.6 hours ahead of deadline, plenty of time to spare—she gave Osthen permission to bring their friends over again. It didn't take long for Osthen to schedule more parties. Kanseun lectured the foxwife endlessly on appropriate behavior at parties, emphasizing that he was to say no to anything uncomfortable and to come get her if anyone got pushy. Osthen's taste in friends wasn't too unreasonable, but she worried.

Osthen's friends, like Osthen, interacted genially enough with the foxwife when in his presence (and hers). However, they never seemed to remember him once they left the apartment, as Kanseun discovered when she ran into Osthen's latest lover at one of the cafeterias. This applied even when Kanseun, in a fit of experimentation, brought the foxwife with her. The foxwife, for his part, was attentive to the points of etiquette that Kanseun had instructed him in, although she never got him to be less than effervescently polite.

Kanseun would have bought the foxwife some proper clothes. After the first day, however, he made this unnecessary by taking his fashion cues from Osthen. (Except for the spectacles. He always wore the spectacles.) She assumed that the lookalike designer clothes came from the same nowhere place as items like the broom. The one time she asked him about it, he attributed it to his superior organizational skills. How "organizational skills" accounted for the spontaneous generation of matter, she wasn't sure, but as long as no one turned up looking for lost items she didn't much care.

She came home once to find that he was beating wrinkles out of Osthen's clothes, using wooden beaters and some kind of primitive board. It took days for her to explain the extent of the chores that he did not, in fact, have to do by hand. And afterward she would still catch him doing them, and have to drag him away until the next time.

The foxwife was very good at video games. He was especially fond of the ones with hyperrealistic gouts of blood, but she had to console him every time he failed a mission and one of the game allies died, even when she explained to him that the game was fictional and you could restore saved games and, occasionally, resurrect characters. He'd curl up against her shoulder and sob quietly, dabbing at his eyes with a red-and-white polka-dotted handkerchief, before trying again.

He also had a great disdain for tigers—he called them "amateurs"— but would not say why. It wasn't as if the station housed anything as exotic or dangerous as tigers, and it only came up because Osthen mentioned the visiting dreadnought *Tigertooth*.

The one time Osthen managed to step on a stray nail in a bad way, the foxwife talked them into letting him remove the thing. Kanseun wasn't sure how she resisted the temptation to find a bomb to see if the foxwife could disarm it. She hoped it never became relevant. Even so, she couldn't escape the disquieting thought: where would he have acquired such a skill?

Another letter arrived. Kanseun immediately put it in the pile with the others before the foxwife could file it for her, and then wondered why she was so embarrassed at the thought of him catching her doing this. This one, too, went unread and unanswered.

The foxwife's obsession with doing chores continued to bother Kanseun. She finally discussed the matter with Osthen.

"Do *you* think I should try to get him to talk to a counselor?" Kanseun said in a low voice. The foxwife was in the kitchen. She didn't know how good his hearing was, so she'd turned up the entertainment system. It was currently playing some hot new null-gravity sport and she was trying not to watch. Sure, she'd undergone the necessary safety training upon moving here, but she was a stereotypical planetsider and she *liked* gravity.

"I don't mind him living here," Osthen said. They didn't look up from the miniature they were painting. "I mean, it's not like he takes up more space than my junk does. He fits nicely on the couch at night. And he seems happy, doesn't he?"

There was a certain degree of unreality to any conversation about the foxwife, given Osthen's on-off ability to remember his existence.

"But don't you think he deserves better?" Kanseun said.

"Better according to who?" Osthen retorted. "If this is so important to you, why aren't you discussing it with him? Find out what he wants for himself?"

She couldn't think of any noncondescending way to say *Because I don't think he's healthy enough to decide for himself.*

"Is it because you think he's mentally tilted?" they said. She'd forgotten that Osthen, for all their laziness, could be good at reading people when they wanted to. Even if that was why she was asking their advice in the first place. "Because it's still his life and still his say. Unless you're planning to break up with him over it."

Kanseun gritted her teeth. "We're not dating. It's not my fault he goes around calling himself a foxwife."

Osthen did look up then, and their eyes were sharp and not a little disappointed. "If he calls himself a foxwife, he *is* a foxwife."

"Not literally he isn't." Inexplicable abilities, yes. But he couldn't be a mythological figure. He was real.

They shrugged and dabbed their brush into the pot of steel-blue paint. "So? You're still talking to the wrong person."

"You're no help," Kanseun snapped, and regretted it immediately.

Osthen had gone into "there's no reasoning with you" mode and had returned their attention to the miniature. She wasn't going to get anything else out of them tonight, and it was all her damn fault.

She glanced toward the kitchen to see if the foxwife was still puttering around; froze. He was standing in the doorway, staring at her, red-and-white polka-dotted handkerchief scrunched up in his hand.

Kanseun opened her mouth.

The foxwife walked past her and out of the apartment.

She lunged after him; of course she did. But no sooner had she reached out to grab his shoulder than he wasn't there. She almost fell over. What else had she expected from someone who could turn himself into a table?

"Did you see where he went?" Kanseun said to Osthen.

"He who?" Osthen said.

Her heart turned to needles. "I have to look for him," she said reflexively, and all but ran out the door herself.

Kanseun spent the rest of the day and most of the night searching the station. She stopped by one of the ubiquitous kiosks, asking after someone of the foxwife's description, although it came as no surprise that the kiosk said, patiently, that no such person had asked for help. There was no sign of him at any of the cheap cafes or restaurants she had taken him to before, or even some of the ones they'd never gone to together.

Reasoning (hoping, more likely) that he would stick to the university level, she returned there and began knocking on doors. Not everyone answered, but those who did were unfailingly polite in their demurrals, which she took as a side-effect of the foxwife's unchanciness. No, they hadn't seen the boy she was looking for. In fact, they'd never seen anyone like that at all. And who wore spectacles these days, anyway?

Wrung out, eyes stinging, she finally conceded defeat at four in the morning. She'd go out tomorrow and try again. Osthen had already gone to bed. She looked around at the jacket that Osthen had kicked into a corner and went to pick it up and fold it away, even though she never picked up after her roommate. Then she sat down on the couch. Her head started to pound, and it took a long time for sleep to come.

The next morning—more like very early afternoon, since she wasn't used to having her sleep this messed up—Kanseun went to the kitchen to look at the teas directly because the watcher's voice aggravated her lingering headache and she didn't want it to enumerate all the options. She found the foxwife in the kitchen, eating ginger peach jam directly out of the jar.

Kanseun didn't lecture him about it.

The foxwife didn't say anything at all.

She pulled up a stool and sat next to him, watching him eat. The spoon wasn't one of hers.

After a moment, he produced another one and offered it to her. Kanseun accepted it gravely. It was beautiful: made of some beaten bronzy metal, maybe even actual bronze. There was a little curled fox engraved on the handle.

The foxwife held out the jar. Kanseun dipped the spoon in and had a mouthful of jam. It tasted delicious, like honed sunlight.

They finished the jam together, in companionable silence.

Two weeks and one day after that, the latest letter arrived for Kanseun. More specifically, it arrived while she and the foxwife were out for a walk. When they returned, the watcher said, "You have correspondence from your older father." Today its voice was bright, Osthen's latest fancy. "I have left it on your desk."

Kanseun had been in a good mood, which evaporated when she realized how long she had been avoiding the letters. "Great," she said, and made no move toward her desk.

The foxwife's organizational instincts had been triggered, however, and he went to pick it up. "Shall I open it for you?" he asked.

"Go ahead," she said with a sigh. "I'm impressed Older Father even bothers when I'm such a lousy correspondent."

The foxwife produced a letter opener, although he could have used the one she kept on her desk, and slit the envelope open. He held it up and looked intently at it. She thought he was admiring the calligraphy— Older Father did beautiful work, elegant rhythmic strokes, even if she struggled to decipher it—until he said, "It says there's been a lot of rain in the city, and are you studying hard still, and—"

"You can read this?" Kanseun said. She didn't know why she was so surprised, given the foxwife's proven facility with languages. Maybe it was the fact that he was holding the letter sideways.

Nevertheless, he started reading: "'On this 23rd of 11-month in the year 4297 of the Azalea Cycle'—"

"Wait, wait, wait," she said. "I thought you didn't do numbers." She hadn't meant it to come out like a put-down.

"4297 comes after 4296 and before 4298," the foxwife said. Misinterpreting her confusion, he added, with a hint of dismay, "If you want me to do all the numbers in between 4296 and 4297, and 4297 and 4298, we're going to be here a long time. As in infinitely long . . . "

"Remember when we first met," Kanseun said slowly, "and I asked how many people, and—?" She held out her hands the way he had. Thought of the foxwife holding up his fingers one by one.

"Yes," he said, and looked away. "I stopped counting after ten thousand or so."

Ten *thousand*. Kanseun swallowed. "How long have you been doing this?"

"A very long time," the foxwife said. He took off his spectacles and tapped the frame, a nervous tic she had never seen before. His eyes had gone sad and dark. "I'm the last of my litter. There were more of us once. I wasn't—I'm not a good foxwife. The sister who raised me was a very proper foxwife. According to the family stories, she seduced queens and investment bankers and fighter pilots, and she collected eggs made of gold wire and glass, and she insisted that I learn mathematics so I wouldn't get cheated in the stock market.

"She told me once that being a foxwife is all about shapeshifting. I tried to do as she said, but we got separated when we started following our humans off the origin world. I'm only good at things like tables and vases and fountain pens, not the kinds of shapeshifting that matter."

He lifted his chin and put the spectacles back on. "But there's no help for it," he said. This time his bright tone didn't fool her. "I have to do what I can to be useful in the world as it exists, that's all."

Kanseun regarded him intently. "Listen," she said. "How much of my language do you read?"

"All of it, I expect," the foxwife said unboastfully. "My family believed in the value of a good education."

"Do you write it too?"

He was smiling at her. "Yes," he said. "Yes."

"Teach me," Kanseun said. "I won't pretend I'm good at languages, but if I work at it and you're patient with me, I might pick something up." The next words came out in a rush: "Older Father used to tell me fox stories, shapechanger stories. I don't know if they're about your people, or about something else. But I could—I could ask him. Maybe he would know something." Maybe even something that would help the foxwife find his sister. "Of course, if I wait until I know enough Na-ahn to formulate the question, it could be a while, so I should just ask in Kestran—"

11

She'd been avoiding Older Father's letters for months now. What if he said something reproving, or worse, simply forgave her? What if he didn't remember the fox stories at all? What if, what if, what if. But she looked at the foxwife and thought, *Ten thousand doors. I can try, too.*

"I'm sure he would be happy to hear from you either way," the foxwife said. "But we can start the lessons whenever you want."

"Today," Kanseun said. "Let's start today."

ABOUT THE AUTHOR

Yoon Ha Lee's works have appeared in *Lightspeed, Tor.com, Beneath Ceaseless Skies,* and *The Magazine of Fantasy and Science Fiction.* Her collection *Conservation of Shadows* came out in 2013 from Prime Books. Currently she lives in Louisiana with her family and has not yet been eaten by gators.

Stone Hunger

N. K. JEMISIN

Once there was a girl who lived in a beautiful place full of beautiful people who made beautiful things. Then the world broke.

Now the girl is older, and colder, and hungrier. From the shelter of a dead tree, she watches as a city—a rich one, big, with high strong walls and well-guarded gates—winches its roof into place against the falling chill of night. The girl has never seen anything like this city's roof. She's watched the city for days, fascinated by its ribcage of metal tracks and the strips of sewn, oiled material they pull along it. They must put out most of their fires when they do this, or they would choke on smoke—but perhaps with the strips in place, the city retains warmth enough to make fires unnecessary.

It will be nice to be warm again. The girl shifts her weight from one fur-wrapped thigh to the other, her only concession to anticipation.

The tree in whose skeletal branches she crouches is above the city, on a high ridge, and it is one of the few still standing. The city has to burn something, after all, and the local ground does not have the flavor of coal-land, sticky veins of pent smoky bitterness lacing through cool bedrock. In the swaths of forest the city-dwellers have taken, even the stumps are gone; nothing wasted. The rest has been left relatively unmolested, though the girl has noted a suspicious absence of deadfall and kindling-wood on the shadowed forest floor below. Perhaps they've left this stand of trees as a windbreak, or to keep the ridge stable. Whatever their reasons, the city-dwellers' forethought works in her favor. They will not see her stalking them, waiting for an opportunity, until it is too late.

And perhaps, if she is lucky—

No. She has never been lucky. The girl closes her eyes again, tasting the land and the city. It is the most distinctive city she has ever encountered. Such a complexity of sweets and meats and bitters and . . . sour.

Hmm.

Perhaps.

The girl settles her back against the trunk of the tree, wraps the tattered blanket from her pack more closely around herself, and sleeps.

Dawn comes as a thinning of the gray sky. There has been no sun for years.

The girl wakes because of hunger: a sharp pang of it, echo of long-ago habit. Once, she ate breakfast in the mornings. Unsated, the pang eventually fades to its usual omnipresent ache.

Hunger is good, though. Hunger will help.

The girl sits up, feeling imminence like an intensifying itch. *It's coming.* She climbs down from the tree—easily; handholds were gnawed into the trunk by ground animals in the early years, before that species disappeared—and walks to the edge of the ridge. Dangerous to do this, stand on a ridge with a shake coming, but she needs to scout for an ideal location. Besides; she knows the shake isn't close. Yet.

There.

The walk down into the valley is more difficult than she expects. There are no paths. She has to half-climb, half-slide down dry runnels in the rock face which are full of loose gravel-sized ash. And she is not at her best after starving for eight days. Her limbs go weak now and again. There will be food in the city, she reminds herself, and moves a little faster.

She makes it to the floor of the valley and crouches behind a cluster of rocks near the half-dried-up river. The city gates are still hundreds of feet away, but there are familiar notches along its walls. Lookouts, perhaps with longviewers; she knows from experience that cities have the resources to make good glass—and good weapons. Any closer and they'll see her, unless something distracts them.

Once there was a girl who waited. And then, at last, the distraction arrives. A shake.

The epicenter is not nearby. That's much farther north: yet another reverberation of the rivening that destroyed the world. Doesn't matter. The girl breathes hard and digs her fingers into the dried riverbed as power rolls toward her. She *tastes* the vanguard of it sliding along her tongue, leaving a residue to savor, like thick and sticky treats—

(It is not real, what she tastes. She knows this. Her father once spoke of it as the sound of a chorus, or a cacophony; she's heard others complain of foul smells, painful sensations. For her, it is food. This seems only appropriate.)

—and it is easy—delicious!—to reach further down. To visualize herself opening her mouth and lapping at that sweet flow of natural force. She sighs and relaxes into the rarity of pleasure, unafraid for once, letting her guard down shamelessly and guiding the energy with only the merest brush of her will. A tickle, not a push. A lick.

Around the girl, pebbles rattle. She splays herself against the ground like an insect, fingernails scraping rock, ear pressed hard to the cold and gritty stone.

Stone. *Stone.*

Stone like gummy fat, like slick warm syrups she vaguely remembers licking from her fingers, stone flowing, pushing, curling, slow and inexorable as toffee. Then this oncoming power, the wave that ripples the stone, stops against the great slab of bedrock that comprises this valley and its surrounding mountains. The wave wants to go around, spend its energy elsewhere, but the girl sucks against this resistance. It takes awhile. On the ground, she writhes in place and smacks her lips and makes a sound: "*Ummmah.*"

Then the

Oh, the pressure

Once there was a girl who ground her teeth against prrrrrresssure *bursts*, the inertia *breaks*, and the wave of force ripples into the valley. The land seems to inhale, rising and groaning beneath her, and it is hers, it's *hers*. She controls it. The girl laughs; she can't help herself. It feels so good to be full, in one way or another.

A jagged crack steaming with friction opens and widens from where the girl lies to the foot of the ridge on which she spent the previous night. The entire face of the cliff splits off and disintegrates, gathering momentum and strength as it avalanches toward the city's southern wall. The girl adds force in garnishing dollops, oh-so-carefully. Too much and she will smash the entire valley into rubble, city and all, leaving nothing useful. She does not destroy; she merely damages. But just enough and—

The shake stops.

The girl feels the interference at once. The sweet flow solidifies; something taints its flavor in a way that makes her recoil. Hints of bitter and sharp—

—and *vinegar*, at last, for certain, she isn't imagining it this time, *vinegar*—

—and then all the marvelous power she has claimed dissipates. There is no compensatory force; nothing *uses* it. It's simply gone. Someone else has beaten her to the banquet and eaten all the treats. But the girl no longer cares that her plan has failed.

"I found you." She pushes herself up from the dry riverbed, her hair dripping flecks of ash. She is trembling, not just with hunger anymore, her eyes fixed on the city's unbroken wall. "*I found you.*"

The momentum of the shake rolls onward, passing beyond the girl's reach. Though the ground has stopped moving, the ridge rockslide cannot be stopped: boulders and trees, including the tree that sheltered the girl the night before, break loose and tumble down to slam against the city's protective wall, probably cracking it. But this is nowhere near the level of damage that the girl had hoped for. How will she get inside? She *must* get inside, now.

Ah—the gates of the city crank open. A way in. But the city dwellers are angry now. They might kill her, or worse.

She rises, runs. The days without food have left her little strength and poor speed, but fear supplies some fuel. Yet the stones turn against her now, and she stumbles, slips on loose rocks. She knows better than to waste time looking back.

Hooves drum the ground, a thousand tiny shakes that refuse to obey her will.

Once there was a girl who awoke in a prison cell.

It's dark, but she can see the metal grate of a door not far off. The bed is softer than anything she's slept on in months, and the air is warm. Or *she* is warm. She evaluates the fever that burns under her skin and concludes that it is dangerously high. She's not hungry, either, though her belly is as empty as ever. A bad sign.

This may have something to do with the fact that her leg aches like a low, monotonous scream. Two screams. Her upper thigh burns, but the knee feels as though shards of ice have somehow inserted themselves into the joint. She wants to try and flex it, see if it can move enough to bear her weight, but it hurts so much already that she is afraid to try.

She remains still, listening before opening her eyes, a habit that has saved her life before. Distant sound of voices, echoing along corridors that stink of rust and mildewed mortar. No breath or movement nearby. Sitting up carefully, the girl touches the cloth that covers her. Scratchy, patchy. Warmer than her own blanket, wherever that is. She will steal this one, if she can, when she escapes.

Then she freezes, startled, because there is someone in the room with her. A man.

But the man does not move, does not even breathe; just stands there. And now she can see that what she thought was skin is marble. A statue. A statue?

It's hard to think through the clamor of fever and pain, even the air sounds loud in her ears, but she decides at last that the city-dwellers have peculiar taste in art.

She hurts. She's tired. She sleeps.

"You tried to kill us," says a woman's voice.

The girl blinks awake again, disoriented for a moment. A lantern burns something smoky in a sconce above her. Her fever has faded. She's still thirsty, but not as parched as before. A memory comes to her of people in the room, tending her wounds, giving her broth tinged with bitterness; this memory is distant and strange. She must have been half delirious at the time. She's still hungry—she is always hungry—but that need, too, is not as bad as it was. Even the fire and ice in her leg have subsided.

The girl turns to regard her visitor. The woman sits straddling an old wooden chair, her arms propped on its back. The girl does not have enough experience of other people to guess her age. Older than herself; not elderly. And big, with broad shoulders made broader by layers of clothing and fur, heavy black boots. Her hair, a poufing mane as gray and stiff as ash-killed grass, has been thickened further by plaits and knots which are either decoration or an attempt to keep the mass of it out of her eyes. Her face is broad and angular, her skin sallow-brown like the girl's own.

(The statue that was in the corner is gone. Once there was a girl who hallucinated while in a fever.)

"You would've torn down half our southern wall," the woman continues. "Probably destroyed one or more storecaches. That kind of thing is enough to kill a city these days. Wounds draw scavengers."

This is true. It would not have been her intention, of course. She tries to be a successful parasite, not killing off her host; she inflicts only enough damage to get inside undetected. And while the city was busy repairing itself and fighting off the enemies who would have come, the girl could have survived unnoticed within its walls for some time. She has done this elsewhere. She could have prowled its alleys, nibbled at its foundations, searching always for the taste of vinegar. *He is here somewhere.*

And if she fails to find him in time, if he does to this city what he has done elsewhere . . . well. She would not kill a city herself, but she'll fatten herself off the carcass before she takes up his trail again. Anything else would be wasteful.

The woman waits a moment, then sighs as if she expected no response. "I'm Ykka. I assume you have no name?"

17

"Of course I have a name," the girl snaps.

Ykka waits. Then she snorts. "You look, what, fourteen? Underfed, so let's say eighteen. You were a small child when the Rivening happened, but you're not feral now—much—so someone must have raised you for awhile afterward. Who?"

The girl turns away in disinterest. "You going to kill me?"

"What will you do if I say yes?"

The girl sets her jaw. The walls of her cell are panels of steel bolted together, and the floor is joined planks of wood over a dirt floor. But such *thin* metal. So *little* wood. She imagines squeezing her tongue between the slats of the floor, licking away the layers of filth underneath—she's eaten worse—and finally touching the foundation. Concrete. Through that, she can touch the valley floor. The stone will be flavorless and cold, cold enough to make her tongue stick, because there's nothing to heat it up—no shake or aftershake. And the valley is nowhere near a fault or hotspot, so no blows or bubbles, either. But there are other ways to warm stone. Other warmth and movement she can use.

Using the warmth and movement of the air around her, for example. Or the warmth and movement within a living body. If she takes this from Ykka, it won't give her much. Not enough for a real shake; she would need more people for that. But she might be able to jolt the floor of her cell, warp that metal door enough to jiggle the lock free. Ykka will be dead, but some things cannot be helped.

The girl reaches for Ykka, her mouth watering in spite of herself—

A clashing flavor interrupts her. Spice like cinnamon. Not so bad. But the bite of the spice grows sharper as she tries to grasp the power, until suddenly it is fire and *burning* and a crisp green taste that makes her eyes water and her guts churn—

With a gasp, the girl snaps her eyes open. The woman smiles, and the back of the girl's neck prickles with belated, jarring recognition.

"Answer enough," Ykka says lightly, though there is cold fury in her eyes. "We'll have to move you to a better cell if you have the sensitivity to work through steel and wood. Lucky for us you've been too weak to try before now." She pauses. "If you had succeeded just now, would you have only killed me? Or the whole city?"

Still shocked to find herself in the company of her own, the girl answers honestly before she can think not to. "Not the whole city. I don't kill cities."

"What is that, some kind of integrity?" Ykka snorts a laugh.

There's no point in answering the question. "I would've just killed as many people as I needed to get loose."

"And then what?"

The girl shrugs. "Find something to eat. Somewhere warm to hole up." She does not add, *find the vinegar man.* It will make no sense to Ykka anyway.

"Food, warmth, and shelter. Such simple wants." There is mockery in Ykka's voice, and it annoys the girl. "You could do with fresh clothes. A good wash. Someone to talk to, maybe, so you can start thinking of other people as valuable."

The girl scowls. "What do you want from me?"

"To see if you're useful." At the girl's frown, Ykka looks her up and down, perhaps sizing her up. The girl does not have the same bottlebrush hair as Ykka, just scraggling brown stuff she chops off with her knife whenever it gets long enough to annoy. She is small and lean and quick, when she is not injured. No telling what Ykka thinks of these traits. No telling why she cares. The girl just hopes she does not appear weak.

"Have you done this to other cities?" Ykka asks.

The question is so patently stupid that there's no point in answering. After a moment Ykka nods. "Thought so. You seem to know what you're about."

"I learned early how it was done."

"Oh?"

The girl decides she has said enough. But before she can make a point of silence, there is another ripple across her perception, followed by something that is unmistakably a jolt within the earth. Specks of mortar trickle from beneath a loose panel on the cell wall. Another shake? No, the deep earth is still cold. That jolt was more shallow, delicate, just a goosebump on the world's skin.

"You can ask what that was," Ykka says, noticing her confusion. "I might even answer."

The girl sets her jaw and Ykka laughs, getting to her feet. She is even bigger than she seemed while sitting, a solid six feet or more. Pureblooded Sanzed; half the races of the world have that bottlebrush hair, but the size is the giveaway. Sanzed breed for strength, so they can protect themselves when the world turns hard.

"You left the southern ridge unstable," Ykka says. "We needed to make repairs." Then she waits, one hand on her hip, while the girl makes the necessary connections. It doesn't take long. The woman is like her. (Taste of savory pepper stinging her mouth still. Disgusting.) But someone entirely different caused that shift a moment ago, and although their presence is like melon—pale, delicate, flavorlessly cloying—it holds a faint aftertaste of blood.

Two in one city? Their kind know better. Hard enough for one wolf to hide among the sheep. But wait—there were two more, right when she split the southern ridge. One of them was a different taste altogether, bitter, something she has never eaten so she cannot name it. The other was the vinegar man.

Four in one city. And this woman is so very interested in her usefulness. She stares at Ykka. No one would do that.

Ykka shakes her head, amusement fading. "I think you're a waste of time and food," she says, "but it's not my decision alone. If you try to harm the city again we'll feel it, and we'll stop you, and then we'll kill you. But if you don't cause trouble, we'll know you're at least trainable. Oh—and stay off the leg if you ever want to walk again."

Then Ykka goes to the grate-door and barks something in another language. A man comes down the hall and lets her out. The two of them look in at the girl for a long moment before heading down the hall and through another door.

In the new silence, the girl sits up. This must be done slowly; she is very weak. Her bedding reeks of fever sweat, though it is dry now. When she throws off the patch-blanket, she sees that she has no pants on. There is a bandage around her right thigh at the midpoint: the wound underneath radiates infection-lines, though they seem to be fading. Her knee has also been wrapped tightly with wide leather bandages. She tries to flex it and a sickening ripple of pain radiates up and down the leg, like aftershocks from her own personal rivening. What did she do to it? She remembers running from people on horseback. Falling, amid rocks as jagged as knives.

The vinegar man will not linger long in this city. She knows this from having tracked his spoor for years. Sometimes there are survivors in the towns he's murdered, who—if they can be persuaded to speak—tell of the wanderer who camped outside the gates, asking to be let in but not moving on when refused. Waiting, perhaps for a few days; hiding if the townsfolk drove him away. Then strolling in, smug and unmolested, when the walls fell. She has to find him quickly because if he's here, this city is doomed, and she doesn't want to be anywhere near its death throes.

Continuing to push against the bandages' tension, the girl manages to bend the knee perhaps twenty degrees before something that should not move that way slides to one side. There is a wet *click* from somewhere within the joint. Her stomach is empty. She is glad for this as she almost retches from the pain. The heaves pass. She will not be escaping the room, or hunting down the vinegar man, anytime soon.

But when she looks up, someone is in the room with her again. The statue she hallucinated.

It *is* a statue, her mind insists—though, plainly, it is not a hallucination. Study of a man in contemplation: tall, gracefully poised, the head tilted to one side with a frank and thoughtful expression moulded into its face. That face is marbled gray and white, though inset with eyes of—she guesses—alabaster and onyx. The artist who sculpted this creation has applied incredible detail, even carving lashes and little lines in the lips. Once, the girl knew beauty when she saw it.

She also thinks that the statue was not present a moment ago. In fact, she's certain of this.

"Would you like to leave?" the statue asks, and the girl scrambles back as much as her damaged leg—and the wall—allows.

There is a pause.

"S-stone-eater," she whispers.

"Girl." Its lips do not move when it speaks. The voice comes from somewhere within its torso. The stories say that the stuff of a stone-eater's body is not quite rock, but still far different from—and less flexible than—flesh.

The stories also say that stone-eaters do not exist, except in stories about stone-eaters. The girl licks her lips.

"What . . . " Her voice breaks. She pulls herself up straighter and flinches when she forgets her knee. It very much does not want to be forgotten. She focuses on other things. "Leave?"

The stone-eater's head does not move, but its eyes shift ever-so-slightly. Tracking her. She has the sudden urge to hide under the blanket to escape its gaze, but then what if she peeks out and finds the creature right in front of her, peering back in?

"They'll move you to a more secure cell, soon." It is shaped like a man, but her mind refuses to apply the pronoun to something so obviously not human. "You'll have a harder time reaching stone there. I can take you to bare ground."

"Why?"

"So that you can destroy the city, if you still want to." Casual, calm, its voice. It is indestructible, the stories say. One cannot stop a stone-eater, only get out of its way.

"You'll have to fight Ykka and the others, however," it continues. "This is their city, after all."

This is almost enough to distract the girl from the stone-eater's looming strangeness. "No one would do that," she says, stubborn. The world hates what she is; she learned that early on. Those of her kind eat the power of the earth and spit it back as force and destruction. When the earth is quiet they eat anything else they can find—the warmth of the air, the movement of living things—to achieve the same effect. They cannot live among ordinary people. They would be discovered with the first shake, or the first murder.

The stone-eater moves, and seeing this causes chilly sweat to rise on the girl's skin. It is slow, stiff. She hears a faint sound like the grind of a tomb's cover-stone. Now the creature faces her, and its thoughtful expression has become wry.

"There are twenty-three of you in this city," it says. "And many more of the other kind, of course." Ordinary people, she guesses by its dismissive tone. Hard to tell, because her mind has set its teeth in that first sentence. Twenty-three. *Twenty-three.*

Belatedly, she realizes the stone-eater is still waiting for an answer to its question. "H-how would you take me out of the cell?" she asks.

"I'd carry you."

Let the stone-eater touch her. She tries not to let it see her shudder, but its lips adjust in a subtle way. Now the statue has a carved, slight smile. The monster is amused to be found monstrous.

"I'll return later," it says. "When you're stronger."

Then its form, which does not vibrate on her awareness the way people do but is instead as still and solid as a mountain—shimmers. She can see through it. It drops into the floor as though a hole has opened under its feet, although the grimy wooden slats are perfectly solid.

The girl takes several deep breaths and sits back against the wall. The metal is cold through her clothing.

They move the girl to a cell whose floor is wood over metal. The walls are wood too, and padded with leather sewn over thick layers of cotton. There are chains set into the floor here, but thankfully they do not use them on her.

They bring the girl food: broth with yeast flakes, coarse flat cakes that taste of fungus, sprouted grains wrapped in dried leaves. She eats and grows stronger. After several days have passed, during which the girl's digestive system begins cautiously working again, the guards give her crutches. While they watch, she experiments until she can use them reliably, with minimal pain. Then they bring her to a room where naked people scrub themselves around a shallow pool of circulating steaming water. When she has finished bathing, the guards card her hair for lice. (She has none. Lice come from being around other people.) Finally they give her clothing: undershorts, loose pants of some sort of plant fiber, a second tighter pair of pants made of animal skin, two shirts, a bra she's too scrawny to need, fur-lined shoes. She dons it all, greedily. It's nice to be warm.

They bring her back to her cell, and the girl climbs carefully into the bed. She's stronger, but still weak; she tires easily. The knee cannot bear her weight yet. The crutches are worse than useless—she cannot *sneak* anywhere while noisily levering herself about. The frustration of this chews at her, because the vinegar man is out there, and she fears he will leave—or strike—before she can heal. Yet flesh is flesh, and hers has endured too much of late. It demands its due. She can do nothing but obey.

After she rests for a time, however, she becomes aware that something vast and mountain-still and familiar is in the room again. She opens her eyes to see the stone-eater still and silent in front of the cell's door. This time it has a hand upraised, the palm open and ready. An invitation.

The girl sits up. "Can you help me find someone?"

"Who?"

"A man. A man, like—" She has no idea how to communicate it in a way the stone-eater will understand. Does it even distinguish between one human and another? She has no idea how it thinks.

"Like you?" the stone-eater prompts, when she trails off.

She fights back the urge to immediately reject this characterization. "Another who can do what I do, yes." One of twenty-three. This is a problem she never expected to have.

The stone-eater is silent for a moment. "Share him with me."

The girl does not understand this. But its hand is still there, proffered, waiting, so she pushes herself to her feet and, with the aid of the crutches, hobbles over. When she reaches for its hand, there is an instant in which every part of her revolts against the notion of touching its strange marbled skin. Bad enough to stand near where she can see that it does not breathe, notice that it does not blink, realize her every instinct warns against tasting it with that part of herself that knows stone. She thinks that if she tries, its flavor will be bitter almonds and burning sulfur, and then she will die.

And yet.

Reluctantly, she thinks of the beautiful place, which she has not allowed herself to remember for years. Once upon a time there was a girl who had food every day and warmth all the time, and in that place were people who gave these things to her, unasked, completely free. They gave her other things, too—things she does not want now, does not need anymore, like companionship and a name and feelings beyond hunger and anger. That place is gone, now. Murdered. Only she remains, to avenge it.

She takes the stone-eater's hand. Its skin is cool and yields slightly to the touch; her arms break out in gooseflesh, and the skin of her palm crawls. She hopes it does not notice.

It waits, until she recalls its request. So she closes her eyes and remembers the vinegar man's sharp-sweet taste, and hopes that it can somehow feel this through her skin.

"Ah," the stone-eater says. "I do know that one."

The girl licks her lips. "I'm going to kill him."

"You're going to try." Its smile is a fixed thing.

"Why are you helping me?"

"I told you. The others will fight you."

This makes no sense. "Why don't you destroy the city yourself, if you hate it so much?"

"I don't hate the city. I have no interest in destroying it." Its hand tightens ever-so-slightly, a hint of pressure from the deepest places of the earth. "Shall I take you to him?"

It is a warning, and a promise. The girl understands: she must accept its offer now, or it will be rescinded. And in the end, it doesn't matter why the stone-eater helps her.

"Take me to him," she says.

The stone-eater pulls her closer, folding its free arm around her shoulders with the slow, grinding inexorability of a glacier. She stands trembling against its solid inhumanity, looking into its too-white, too-dark eyes and clutching her crutches tight with her arms. It hasn't ever stopped smiling. She notices, and does not know why she notices, that it smiles with its lips closed.

"Don't be afraid," it says without opening its mouth, and the world blurs around her. There is a stifling sense of enclosure and pressure, of friction-induced heat, a flicking darkness and a feel of deep earth moving around her, so close that she cannot just taste it; she also feels and breathes and *is* it.

Then they stand in a quiet courtyard of the city. The girl looks around, startled by the sudden return of light and cold air and spaciousness, and does not even notice the stone-eater's movements this time as it slowly releases her and steps back. It is daytime. The city's roof is rolled back and the sky is its usual melancholy gray, weeping ashen snow. From inside, the city feels smaller than she'd imagined. The buildings are low but close together, nearly all of them squat and round and dome-shaped. She's seen this style of building in other cities; good for conserving heat and withstanding shakes.

No one else is around. The girl turns to the stone-eater, tense.

24

"There." Its arm is already raised, pointing to a building at the end of a narrow road. It is a larger dome than the rest, with smaller subsidiaries branching off its sides. "He's on the second floor."

The girl watches the stone-eater for a moment longer and it watches her back, a gently-smiling signpost. *That way to revenge.* She turns and follows its pointing finger.

No one notices her as she crutches along, though she is a stranger; this means the city's big enough that not everyone knows everyone else. The people she passes are of many races, many ages. Sanzed like Ykka predominate, or maybe they are Cebaki; she never learned tell one from another. There are many black-lipped Regwo, and one Shearar woman with big moon-pale eyes. The girl wonders if they know of the twenty-three. (Twenty-*four,* her mind corrects.) They must. Her kind cannot live among ordinary people without eventually revealing themselves. Usually they can't live among ordinary people at all—and yet here, somehow, they do.

Yet as she passes narrower streets and gaps in the buildings, she glimpses something else, something worse, that suddenly explains why no one's worried about twenty-four people who each could destroy a city on a whim. In the shadows, on the sidewalks, nearly camouflaged by the ash-colored walls: too-still standing figures. Statues whose eyes shift to follow her. *Many* of them: she counts a dozen before she makes herself stop.

Once there was a city full of monsters, of whom the girl was just another one.

No one stops her from going into the large dome. Inside, this building is warmer than the one in which she was imprisoned. People move in and out of it freely, some in knots of twos and threes, talking, carrying tools or paper. As the girl moves through its corridors, she spies small ceramic braziers in each room which emit a fragrant scent as well as heat. There are stacks of long-dead flowers in the kindling piles.

The stairs nearly kill her. It takes some time to figure out a method of crutching her way up that does not force her to bend the damaged knee. She stops after the third set to lean against a wall, trembling and sweating. The days of steady food have helped, but she is still healing, and she has never been physically strong. It will not do for her to meet the vinegar man and collapse at his feet.

"You all right?"

The girl blinks damp hair out of her eyes. She's in a wide corridor lined by braziers; there is a long, patterned rug—pre-rivening luxury— beneath her feet. The man standing there is as small as she is, which is the only reason she does not react by jerking away from his nearness. He's nearly as pale as the stone-eater, though his skin is truly skin and his hair is stiff because he is probably part Sanzed. He has a cheerful face, which is set in polite concern as he watches her.

And the girl flinches when she instinctively reaches out to taste her surroundings and he tastes of sharp, sour vinegar, the flavor of smelly pickles and old preserved things and wine gone rancid, and it is him, it is *him, she knows his taste.*

"I'm from Arquin," she blurts. The smile freezes on the man's face, making her think of the stone-eater again.

Once there was a city called Arquin, far to the south. It had been a city of artists and thinkers, a beautiful place full of beautiful people, of whom the girl's parents were two. When the world broke—as it often breaks, as the rivening is only the latest exemplary apocalypse of many—Arquin buttoned up against the chill and locked its gates and hunkered down to endure until the world healed and grew warm again. The city had prepared well. Its storecaches were full, its defenses layered and strong; it could have lasted a long time. But then a stranger came to town.

Taut silence, in the wake of the girl's pronouncement.

The man recovers first. His nostrils flare, and he straightens as if to cloak himself in discomfort. "Everyone did what they had to do, back then," he says. "You'd have done it too, if you were me."

Is there a hint of apology in his voice? *Accusation*? The girl bares her teeth. She has not tried to reach the stone beneath the city since she met Ykka. But she reaches now, tracing the pillars in the walls down to the foundation of the building and then deeper, finding and swallowing sweet-mint bedrock cool into herself. There isn't much. There have been no shakes today. But what little power there is is a balm, soothing away the past few days' helplessness and fear.

The vinegar man stumbles back against the corridor's other wall, reacting to the girl's touch on the bedrock as if to an insult. All at once the sourness of him floods forth like spit, trying to revolt her into letting go. She wants to; he's ruining the taste. But she scowls and bites more firmly into the power, making it hers, refusing to withdraw. His eyes narrow.

Someone comes into the corridor from one of the rooms that branch off it. This stranger says something, loudly; the girl registers that he is calling for Ykka. She barely hears the words. Stone dust is in her mouth. The grind of the deep rock is in her ears. The vinegar man presses in, trying again to wrest control from the girl, and the girl hates him for this. How many years has she spent hungry, cold, afraid, because of him? No, no, she does not begrudge him that, not really, not when she has done just as many terrible things, he's completely right to say *you would too, you did too*—but now? Right now, all she wants is power. Is that so much to ask? It's all he's left her.

And she will shake this whole valley to rubble before she lets him take one more thing that is hers.

The rough-sanded wood of the crutches bites into her hands as she bites into imagined stone to brace herself. The earth is still now, its power too deep to reach, and at such times there's nothing left to feed on save the thin gruel of smaller movements, lesser heat. The rose-flavored coals of the nearby braziers. The jerky twitchy strength of limbs and eyes and breathing chests. And, too, she can sup motions for which there are no names: all the infinitesimal floating morsels of the air, all the jittery particles of solid matter. The smaller, fast-swirling motes that comprise these particles.

(Somewhere, outside the earth, there are more people nearby. Other tastes begin to tease her senses: melon, warm beef stew, familiar peppers. The others mean to stop her. She must finish this quickly.)

"Don't you dare," says the vinegar man. The floor shakes, the whole building rattles with the warning force of his rage. Vibrations drum against the girl's feet. "I won't let you—"

He has no chance to finish the warning. The girl remembers soured wine that she once drank after finding it in a crushed Arquin storehouse. She'd been so hungry that she needed something, anything, to keep going. The stuff had tasted of rich malts and hints of fruit. Desperation made even vinegar taste good.

The air in the room grows cold. A circle of frost, radiating out from the girl's feet, rimes the patterned rug. The vinegar man stands within this circle. (Others in the corridor exclaim and back off as the circle grows.) He cries out as frost forms in his hair, on his eyebrows. His lips turn blue; his fingers stiffen. There's more to it than cold: as the girl devours the space between his molecules, the very motion of his atoms, the man's flesh becomes something different, condensing, hardening. In the earth where flavors dwell, he fights; acid burns the girl's throat and roils her belly. Her own ears go numb, and her knee throbs with the cold hard enough to draw tears from her eyes.

But she has swallowed far worse things than pain. And this is the lesson the vinegar man inadvertently taught her when he killed her future, and made her nothing more than a parasite like himself. He is older, crueler, more experienced, perhaps stronger, but survival has never really been the province of the fittest. Merely the hungriest.

•••

Once the vinegar man is dead, Ykka arrives. She steps into the icy circle without fear, though there is a warning-tang of crisp green and red heat when the girl turns to face her. The girl backs off. She can't handle another fight right now.

"Congratulations," Ykka drawls, when the girl pulls her awareness out of the earth and wearily, awkwardly, sits down. (The floor is very cold against her backside.) "Got that out of your system?"

A bit dazed, the girl tries to process the words. A small crowd of people stands in the corridor, beyond the icy circle; they are murmuring and staring at her. A black-haired woman, as small and lithe as Ykka is large and immovable, has entered the circle with Ykka; she goes over to the vinegar man and peers at him as if hoping to find anything left of value. There's nothing, though. The girl has left as much of him as he left of her life, on a long-ago day in a once-beautiful place. He's not even a man anymore, just a gray-brown, crumbly lump of ex-flesh half-huddled against the corridor wall. His face is all eyes and bared teeth, one hand an upraised claw.

Beyond Ykka and the crowd, the girl sees something that clears her thoughts at once: the stone-eater, just beyond the others. Watching her and smiling, statue-still.

"He's dead," the black-haired woman says, turning to Ykka. She sounds more annoyed than angry.

"Yes, I rather thought so," Ykka replies. "So what was that all about?"

The girl belatedly realizes Ykka is talking to her. She is exhausted, physically—but inside, her whole being brims with strength and heat and satisfaction. It makes her lightheaded, and a little giddy, so she opens her mouth to speak and laughs instead. Even to her own ears, the sound is unsteady, unnerving.

The black-haired woman utters a curse in some language the girl does not know and pulls a knife, plainly intending to rid the city of the girl's mad menace. "Wait," Ykka says.

The woman glares at her. "This little monster just killed Thoroa—"

"Wait," Ykka says again, harder, and this time she stares the black-haired woman down until the furious tension in the woman's shoulders sags into defeat. Then Ykka faces the girl again. Her breath puffs in the chilly air when she speaks. "Why?"

The girl can only shake her head. "He owed me."

"Owed you what? Why?"

She shakes her head again, wishing they would just kill her and get it over with.

Ykka watches her for a long moment, her hard face unreadable. When she speaks again, her voice is softer. "You said you learned early how it was done."

The black-haired woman looks sharply at her. "We've all done what we had to, to survive."

"True," said Ykka. "And sometimes those things come back to bite us."

"She killed a citizen of this city—"

"He owed her. How many people do *you* owe, hmm? You want to pretend we don't all deserve to die for some reason or another?"

The black-haired woman does not answer.

"A city of people like us," the girl says. She's still giddy. It would be easy to make the city shake now, vent the giddiness, but that would force them to kill her when for some impossible reason they seem to be hesitating. "It'll never work. They used to hunt us down before the rivening for good reason."

Ykka smiles as though she knows what the girl is feeling. "They hunt us down now, in most places, for good reason. After all, only one of us could have done this." She gestures vaguely toward the north, where a great jagged red-bleeding crack across the continent has destroyed the world. "But maybe if they didn't treat us like monsters, we wouldn't *be* monsters. I want us to try living like people for awhile, see how that goes."

"Going great so far," mutters the black-haired woman, looking at the stone corpse of the vinegar man. Thoroa. Whichever.

Ykka shrugs, but her eyes narrow at the girl. "Someone will probably come looking for you, too, one day."

The girl gazes steadily back, because she has always understood this. She'll do what she has to do, until she can't anymore.

But all at once the girl snaps alert, because the stone-eater is now standing over her. Everyone in the corridor jerks in surprise. None of them saw it move.

"Thank you," it says.

The girl licks her lips, not looking away. One does not turn one's back on a predator. "Welcome." She does not ask why it thanks her.

"And these," Ykka says from beyond the creature, with a sigh which may or may not be resigned, "are our motivation to live together *peacefully*."

Most of the braziers in the corridor are dark, extinguished by the girl in her desperate grab for power. Only the ones at either far end of the corridor, well beyond the ice-circle, remain lit. These silhouette the stone-eater's face—though the girl can easily imagine its carved-marble smile.

Wordlessly Ykka comes over, as does the black-haired woman. They help the girl to her feet, all three of them watching the stone-eater warily. The stone-eater doesn't move, either to impede them or to get out of the way. It just keeps standing there until they carry the girl away. Others in the hall, bystanders who did not choose to flee while monsters battled nearby, file out as well—quickly. This is only partly because the corridor is freezing.

"Are you throwing me out of the city?" the girl asks. They have set her down at the foot of the steps. She fumbles with the crutches because her hands are shaking in delayed reaction to the cold and the near-death experience. If they throw her out now, wounded, she'll die slowly. She would rather they kill her, than face that.

"Don't know yet," Ykka says. "You want to go?"

The girl is surprised to be asked. It is strange to have options. She looks up, then, as a sound from above startles her: they are rolling the city's roof shut against the coming night. As the strips of roofing slide into place, the city grows dimmer, although people move along the streets lighting standing lanterns she did not notice before. The roof locks into place with a deep, echoing snap. Already, without cool outside air blowing through the city, it feels warmer.

"I want to stay," the girl hears herself say.

Ykka sighs. The black-haired woman just shakes her head. But they do not call the guards, and when they hear a sound from upstairs, all three of them walk away together, by unspoken mutual agreement. The girl has no idea where they're going. She doesn't think the other two women do, either. It's just understood that they should all be somewhere else.

Because the girl keeps seeing the corridor they just left, in the moment before they carried her down stairs. She'd glanced back, see. The stone-eater had moved again; it stood beside Thoroa's petrified corpse. Its hand rested on his shoulder, companionably. And this time as it smiled, it flashed tiny, perfect, diamond teeth.

The girl takes a deep breath to banish this image from her mind.

Then she asks of Ykka as they walk, "Is there anything to eat?"

ABOUT THE AUTHOR

N. K. Jemisin is a Brooklyn author whose short fiction and novels have been multiply nominated for the Hugo and the Nebula, shortlisted for the Crawford and the Tiptree, and have won the Locus Award for Best First Novel. Her speculative works range from fantasy to science fiction to the undefinable; her themes include the intersections of race and gender, resistance to oppression, and the coolness of Stuff Blowing Up. She is a member of the Altered Fluid writing group, and a graduate of the Viable Paradise writing workshop. Her latest novel, *The Shadowed Sun*, was published in June 2012 from Orbit Books, and she's hard at work on a new series due to begin in 2014.

Soul's Bargain

JULIETTE WADE

A reading from the Book of Eyn the Wanderer:

In those days there were many who admired Eyn for her divine beauty, no less than for her wildness, forgetting her fierce loyalty to her lover, Sirin the Luck-Bringer. One among these was a mortal, Ruver of Meluara, renowned for his strength and speed. As many times as she rebuffed him, yet Ruver persisted in his suit, until at last, despairing of further talk, Eyn turned her back and resumed her exploration through the orbits of the dark unknown. Ruver followed running, and coming upon her from behind, cried out her name and caught in his bare hand the tips of her wild white hair. Yet Eyn had already cast off her mortal guise, and the touch of her hair struck Ruver dead.

In terrible anger did Eyn bear Ruver's body back, and placing him before Father Varin, demanded his soul be gnashed in flame for this presumption. Yet then did Mother Elinda touch her with a gentling hand, and bid her look back across the distance to the place where Ruver had died. "He did wrong to follow you, yet see how far he reached beyond the deeds of other mortals."

At this, Eyn relented, and gave Ruver's soul to Mother Elinda, who placed him in the heavens as a shining star. Eyn declared, "Let his light serve as a reminder to all mortals that great things may be achieved in the name of love."

As her assistant Irim finished his reading, Pelisma glanced instinctively toward him, but her failing vision could no longer distinguish him from the vague shadows. Even the bright electric lights on the ceiling gave nothing but a faint glimmer. She ached to think that not so long ago, limestone labyrinths had been her playgrounds. Now she had to rub the velvet of the couch she sat on to feel grounded again.

"Groundbreaker, you seem distressed," Irim said. "I couldn't help but think of your deeds when I read this passage this morning. Was I wrong to guess that you're a ward of Eyn?"

Pelisma shook her head. "No, Irim; I am." Though she'd long since lost the habit of attending chapel, her life's work in building this cavern city had been born of love. She cherished her vivid memory of the day the river Trao changed course through a sinkhole and came thundering in at the gate. A heart-shattering, magnificent sight! She'd mustered the citizens, set explosives, and blasted a new outlet to save the city from inundation. In return, the city's Firstmost had appointed her Groundbreaker, and renamed the city of Lake's Gate: Pelismara, in her honor.

Now that she considered it, she hadn't entirely left behind Eyn's inspiration. Surely the goddess would be disappointed in her now, though—bound by her people's adulation and her own blindness into tiny orbits that held nothing but the known.

A light brightened on her right, and she tried not to flinch.

Almost nothing.

"Irim," she asked, "Is there a wysp nearby?"

"Don't worry," said Irim. "That was me; I moved out from between you and the lamp. There's a wysp in the room, but it's currently drifting near the window."

She shoved down the irrational fear and tried to change the subject. "So. What do we have in today's project updates?"

Irim's footsteps walked nearer, while paper rustled softly. "Good news. Building the agricultural scaffolds around openings to the surface has been an unqualified success. With harvest numbers in, it looks like we can abandon those two surface fields that experienced wysp-fire disasters this year, without risking a citywide shortage." He hesitated. "Pelisma, I'm sorry; I didn't mean to mention wysps. I hope I haven't alarmed you."

"No, not really." Wysps were a fact of life. It wasn't their existence that filled her with dread, so much as their new unpredictable behavior—approaching her closely, for no apparent reason. She'd never felt superstitious about floating sparks she could *see*. "Irim," she confessed. "I feel like they're following me."

Irim's hand gently touched her forearm, a habit he'd developed for which she was unreasonably grateful. "Perhaps they follow you out of love," he said. "As Ruver followed Eyn."

"What?" Pelisma glanced toward him, and ended up frowning at shadows. Irim reading from the Books was no surprise—he was kind and devout, qualities she'd always appreciated. But why should he cast her *wysp* problem in religious terms? Unless . . . "Irim," she said, "I hope you don't mind me asking, but are you a sectarian?"

Irim gave a nervous laugh. "Ah, you've got me. Heretic, yes."

"I don't mean *that*. I'm trying to understand what you're saying."

The couch cushion creaked as Irim sat beside her. "Groundbreaker, I—well, you've saved so many lives. I believe it would be natural for souls to be drawn to you."

Souls. Then the rumors about sectarians were true. Imagine the lonely dead, not placed in Elinda's care where they belonged, but taking the form of wysps and drifting through people's lives. Approaching them. *Threatening and killing them?* She shuddered, feeling suddenly as though a pit gaped beneath her feet.

From a rational perspective, she should ask Irim questions, and let him explain how his faith addressed her fears. But right now, she wasn't sure she could handle a theological argument. Losing her eyesight had been difficult enough; lately it seemed she was also losing her composure.

If she couldn't stay rational, she would no longer be worthy of her post—and if she could no longer work for her people, for Pelismara, then what would her life be worth?

"It's kind of you to say so," she said. "I believe I'd like to see my physician about this wysp issue."

"Doctor Olanen?" Irim asked. "Why?"

Pelisma rubbed her fingers over the couch velvet, so solid and certain. A life of cave work had taught her the solid reliability of limestone walls, level rampways and buttresses, atmospheric lamps and ventilators. Wysps were incorporeal, and thus trickier, but they *had* been observed in detail. Tracking their behaviors in the mines and fields had significantly reduced the risk of wysp fires. Since she could no longer make such observations herself, she must ask someone to do it for her. How else could she banish this fear?

Not wishing to insult Irim, she said, "I'd just like to hear his opinion. Please, Irim."

"Of course, Groundbreaker. I'll call him at once."

Pelisma sat still in her brass chair during her doctor's examination, re-analyzing every wysp experience she could recall. In the city-caverns, wysps came and went without harm, and mostly without notice. In the wild cavern systems outside the city boundaries, any wysp appearance spurred quick checks of the methane detectors, but only rarely did they cause explosions. Thinking of it, she could almost feel the tremors in her bones.

Wysps were everywhere; they could appear anywhere, often emerging out of solid rock. But what might *cause* them to appear?

As he had for the last year, Doctor Olanen always began by shining bright lights into her eyes from various directions. Then he checked her chest, back, and neck with gentle hands—the same routine that always left her feeling old and infirm. Shouldn't it have been different this time? She'd told him to look for wysp attraction factors, not heart murmurs!

The doctor's hands moved away, and Irim's breathing quickened. Pelisma sat straighter in her chair, because Groundbreakers didn't bend with bad news.

"Yes, Doctor?"

"Nothing," said Doctor Olanen. "I can't detect any change in your physical condition that might attract wysps. Your general health is excellent, and you'll be happy to hear that your retinal deterioration is slowing."

"Well." She tried to keep her tone light. "Thank Heile for mercy."

Irim touched her forearm, and instantly, she thought of souls. The stars kept to their orbits, so it was written; they cared for themselves far above, beyond the layers of rock and wilderness. Wysps, though, were unpredictable. Not entirely unlike the living . . .

Oh, heavenly Mother Elinda!

Doctor Olanen cleared his throat. "Groundbreaker, are you sure the wysps' behavior changed *after* your vision trouble began?"

"Yes, absolutely sure. Irim would be able to tell you the precise timing. Please, Irim?"

"Of course," said Irim. "The wysps started approaching her closely about two months after the vision loss began restricting her routines. At first we didn't realize the phenomenon was systematic. Only recently did we think back and realize that they'd been drifting in more frequently for some time."

"So you *have* witnessed this yourself," the doctor said. "Not to suggest that our Groundbreaker is imagining things, but—"

"I most certainly have witnessed it." Irim sounded indignant. "Haunting behaviors are well-documented. Have you spoken with the survivors of wysp incidents, Doctor?"

"I've treated plenty of wysp burns," Doctor Olanen replied, brusquely. "They're *hunting* behaviors, and they *are* well documented, but only on the surface. Underground, wysps drift randomly. You're telling me the

Groundbreaker is somehow witnessing an anomaly never recorded in more than two hundred years?"

Irim replied quietly. "In two hundred years, there has been no one like our Groundbreaker."

Pelisma winced.

"Sorry." Irim touched her forearm soothingly, but then hissed in a breath. Even without the faint new glimmer in her sight, she knew wysps were near.

"How many?" she asked.

"Three," said Doctor Olanen. "They're small, but quite—uh, bright."

"They generally are," she agreed. "Are they drifting, or moving closer?"

No one answered. Bodies scuffled, and someone—Irim?—yelped. Pelisma opened her mouth to ask what was happening, but impatience seized her so suddenly she held her breath.

Ridiculous, this whole thing! None of us know anything! What can I do? What do the wysps want? Can they want? I have to do something—have to, just have to figure this out!

A cold stethoscope pressed against her chest. She shuddered, gulped down the feeling and managed to say something without seeming irrational.

"What happened?"

"It's all right," said Irim, sounding shaken. "They're gone now."

Not permanently, she didn't imagine. "Irim, are you hurt?"

"No, Groundbreaker. I tried to block one getting too close to you, and it floated straight through me—may Mother Elinda stay her hand."

"Did any of them touch *me?*"

"No."

"Then why did you assess me again, Doctor?"

"Its proximity seemed to alarm you," Doctor Olanen replied. "Beyond a slightly elevated heart rate, though, everything is normal."

Pelisma took a deep breath, and rubbed the cold brass of her chair. There was no question of uttering the words 'increasing emotional instability' in the presence of her doctor, if he already thought she was imagining things.

"Doctor Olanen, you saw that, I'm sure," Irim said. "Do you feel inclined to alter your professional opinion?"

"I couldn't say based on a single observation," the doctor replied. "I confess, that's not a behavior I've seen before. Wysp burns fall within my expertise, but their behaviors do not. I'd like to report it to a colleague of mine who researches wysps in Herketh. She might be able to shed more light on the problem."

Sudden inspiration brought Pelisma to her feet. "A researcher—perfect! I'll go speak with her."

Irim seemed flustered by the suggestion. "Groundbreaker, why not order her to come to you? If wysps seek you out during the surface voyage, we have no idea what they might do. Caution is recommended."

Until this moment, caution had been all she had. "Irim, it's only five hours travel before we'll be back underground in Herketh, and I've never heard of a wysp entering a moving vehicle. We'll have no cause to clear land or build fires. Besides, I know I'll be safe if you're with me."

"Pelisma—"

She smiled. "I will even let you drive."

At last, some action! This was much better than foundering in anxiety and despair. As Eyn was her witness, she'd prefer to face danger out on the surface, if it meant she was still alive.

Irim was quieter than usual today as he led her out to their vehicle. Nervous about the surface voyage, he said—but recent advances in hover technology meant that floater travel had not been seriously dangerous for a number of years. His reticence felt weightier than that, laden with the unspoken question that now lay between them.

Unbearable. Every second made her more impatient to leave this awkwardness for the adventure of surface travel. Had he known her feelings, Irim would probably have said she was more like Eyn than ever.

Irim helped her out to the edge of the open square, and laid her left hand on the flat cold metal of the floater car while he opened the door.

"Groundbreaker," he said, "are you sure we should be doing this?"

"We must do something, Irim. I don't prefer to wait and see whether a wysp finally sets me on fire."

"Mercy!" Irim said. "That's true enough." He guided her into the passenger's seat.

Pelisma stroked the soft fabric of her seat, and tried to distract herself. "Could you update me on the latest construction, please? How does it look? Is our residence still so lonely?"

"Not quite," Irim replied, with more cheer. "We'll be neighbors with lawyers and judges soon. They've started on the Court columns, and it looks like they'll match our portico. With the shinca trunk lighting up the whole square, I think it will be beautiful."

Pelisma smiled in relief, imagining it. The shinca tree had been what first drew her to this cavern for the residence of the Firstmost and top staff: alone in the center of a flat basin, it pierced through the ceiling stalactites, reaching up toward its branches on the surface far above.

Its silver-white glow sharpened everything around, while its warmth softened the chill of the deep regions.

Once Irim had engaged her seatbelt, he moved across to the driver's side. The other seatbelt clicked, and then the vehicle hummed and lifted. They drove up the rampway to the fourth level.

"Lots of construction here, too," Irim said. "You just wait; this will be the center of town one day."

"Perhaps so," she agreed, but as the vehicle angled up one rampway after another, and the sounds of life and business grew louder, she couldn't help feeling dissatisfied. *Is this all the ambition we have left? To beautify and perfect a confined existence?* It was all the wysps' doing. The fear that now pursued her was the same fear that kept all of Pelismara below ground: a terrifying vision of death by unquenchable flame.

Irim couldn't be right. What possible wrongs could inspire the dead to visit such punishments upon the living? All her studies, and every event in her life converged upon one fundamental truth: that there was nothing so destructive, nor so implacable as nature, and that meant wysps must be a part of it.

She could feel it as they drove out. Yrindonna Forest rippled all around them, trackless except for the radio-transmitting waymarkers that allowed a driver to track direction while skirting dense thickets and enormous trees that could not be safely cleared away. The hiss of vegetation brushing against the floater's roof and windows roused vivid memories of her last surface drive—the time they'd flushed a flock of kanguan, or that graceful, muscular oryen that had leapt out so close to their path . . .

Lulled by the floater's weaving motions, she'd been drifting in and out of sleep for probably two hours when Irim swore.

"Varin's teeth! Oryen!"

The vehicle swerved, flinging her into her seatbelt. They hit something—a horrible crack came from Irim's side of the floater, the vehicle rebounded at a strange angle, and suddenly they were spinning wildly. Pelisma clutched her seat.

Make it stop, make it stop, oh, make it stop!

They slammed side-first into something solid. The windshield shattered, pelting her face, body and hands with chunks of glass.

Pelisma still held on, sick and disoriented, half-choking on the pounding of her heart. Had they really stopped spinning at last? She found her voice.

"Irim?"

Irim didn't answer.

"Irim! Oh, Elinda forbear!" Grief and fear rose as if to drown her, but she forced them down. *No sentimentality, now: his side of the floater was hit twice, but he might not be dead.* She fumbled for her seatbelt, and managed to release it. Reaching across the space between them, she found Irim's leg: warm, sprinkled with chunks of glass. Carefully, she felt her way up his body. He was slumped against the far side of the floater, which had bowed inward.

"Irim, can you hear me? If you can hear me, make a sound."

The only answer was birdsong, wafting in on a cold breeze heavy with the complex scent of invisible green. Irim's neck was wet with blood, but when she probed with her fingers, his neck and skull seemed unbroken.

There was a pulse beneath his jawline.

Pelisma gasped in relief. She should try to bandage the cut, or cuts, on his head . . . No; first, she should radio for help so someone at least knew they were in trouble . . .

She sniffed.

Smoke?

She searched the air with her hands. Intense heat was coming from the rear of the floater, just where the fire extinguisher was supposed to be. Fire—and it was growing fast, which meant wysps would come.

I can't leave Irim here.

Her fingers shook, but by Sirin's grace, the driver-side seatbelt gave her no trouble. Pelisma gulped down panic and turned away, walking her hands across the dashboard to the passenger door. The latch clicked open easily enough, but the door was jammed. She threw her shoulder into it; on her second attempt, it popped open, and she shoved it outward. Already the smoke had her useless eyes stinging. By the time she got back to Irim, the air tasted thick. Coughing, she worked his nearer leg out of the seat, pulled at his arm and squatted to get him over her shoulders. Grip assured, she put her legs into getting him out. Some part of him was stuck; she heaved until her knees shook.

Sweet Heile, don't let me break him . . .

At last he came free, and she fell face-first into the passenger's seat.

She lay, panting and wheezing into the cloth. It was almost better here, but worse disaster was coming, and they might have only seconds. Thank heavens Irim was not a large man. Pelisma lifted him, but couldn't stand—only managed to flop the two of them out the door into the brush. Bushy vegetation scratched at her face and hands, but the air was breathable. She wriggled out from under Irim and hauled at him again. Won them maybe a foot. Hauled again. A little more.

The fire was now a dreadful wall of heat, crackling and popping as it advanced. Surely it had already ignited whatever vines and leaves were about, possibly also the tree that they had struck. She fought for a better grip under Irim's shoulders and surged backward, two steps, three, four, then turned her ankle and fell with Irim's body across her legs.

She lay, chest heaving, limbs throbbing, waiting for death to find them.

All at once, the fire went out.

Wysps. Pelisma held her breath.

It was an eerie inverse of explosions underground. The wall of heat had vanished, as if sucked straight out of the universe. There was no more wild shapeless light; the hissing and popping had stopped. Pelisma put her arms around Irim as best she could. He was the one who had first explained to her the pattern of the survivor tales: having extinguished a wildfire, wysps could grow a hundredfold—not merely identifying anyone close enough to have caused it, but pursuing them mercilessly and punishing them with flame, while leaving the wilderness untouched.

On the surface, wysps ruled absolutely.

She couldn't hold her breath any longer. She surrendered, breathing in loud gasps. Maybe she should have been angry to be delivered to the mercy of the wysps just when progress had seemed within reach, but all she could feel was remorse. For Irim—thoughtful, faithful Irim, lying here in her lap about to die because of her own rashness.

A flicker came into her vision. Not just a shift in the trees overhead, because it grew brighter, until her eyes filled with light. Mercy—if she could see the wysps so well, imagine how big they must be! She tensed for the oncoming flames. Remorse swelled beyond measure, flooding her, drowning her.

Oh Irim I'm so so sorry how could I have brought this upon you?

Irim groaned.

"Irim!" She sat convulsively, patting over his head, shoulders, and back as if to fight the wysp-flame—but there was none. "Irim," she cried. "Irim, are you all right?"

The weight of his head lifted. "Pelism . . ." It turned into a sigh, and he fell back into her lap. But he wasn't screaming. There were no flames, and the light in her vision faded again to shadow.

The wysps had spared them. But why?

In the forest, there were no reasons. The ground felt like solid ice, leaching heat through her too-thin clothes. The air was a turbulent ocean of sound, in which she could detect nothing familiar. Pelisma rocked back and forth, stroking Irim's head. He was unconscious again, but he was warm. He was solid.

She was less so. Remorse, panic, hope and despair shuddered through her in waves.

Help us, o Wanderer, don't let us die here; bless our path, and show us a way to return!

What if a predator smells our blood?

Elinda, don't take Irim from me! What will I do without him?

That sound—could it be a vehicle? No, it must have been a bird's wings . . .

After a thousand such waves, she could scarcely find words in her head to describe the tides overwhelming her reason. The air darkened, and the temperature continued to drop.

We're going to die . . .

"Irim," Pelisma called, shaking him. "Irim, please."

Still, he didn't answer. She leaned over him, sobbing, until she was too exhausted to continue. Long shuddering breaths didn't seem enough to pull her fully together.

What had become of her ability to stay rational in the worst of situations? Even facing the cascade and the destruction of her city, she'd been all focus, all action. But she had to face up to the truth. Since the blindness—really, since the wysp problem—she'd been increasingly emotional. Maybe this was age affecting her mind . . .

No, you can't afford to say that. You're not dead so long as you can still think.

Why hadn't she thought of it before? Yrindonna forest was vast, and not all of its trees were cold. Shinca trees, too, had their crowns here, and those gave off warmth in every season.

Though logic suggested there must be one somewhere nearby, she felt no evidence of heat in the air. Swirling breezes made it impossible to be sure what lay beyond the reach of her hands. That meant she'd have to search, in such a way that she wouldn't lose Irim. She shifted his weight off her legs, and instantly felt ten times colder.

How can I leave him? What if I can't find him again? He'll die! I can't let Irim die—

Irim moaned.

"Irim!" she cried. "Can you hear me?"

"Pelisma . . . ?"

"Oh, blessing of Heile. We need to move, Irim, or we'll freeze. Can you move?"

He grunted. "I . . . can try. Where to?"

"Tell me if you can see the light of a shinca crown anywhere near."

Irim was silent for several seconds. "Yes. I do."

"But?"

He panted a moment. "You know, we will have been expected in Herketh by now. They'll have sent back a radiogram and the Firstmost will send searchers to our last registered waymarker . . . "

"Irim . . . " She reached for his hand, and found it, sticky with blood. "I'm not sure we have time to wait."

He made an uncomfortable sound. "Shinca crowns attract wysps. More than you ever see in the city-caverns."

More chances to roll the same deadly dice. "Irim, the wysps have left us alive so far," she said. "Maybe—" She took a deep breath. "Maybe we should consider that their mercy."

That silenced him. Finally he said, "All right."

On their first attempt to get him up, Pelisma lost her balance and nearly landed on top of him. Picking herself up for a second attempt, she braced herself better; Irim hissed in pain but managed to stand, leaning against her shoulder. They stumbled along for a few feet, but then she turned her bad ankle on a stone and fell to hands and knees, nearly bringing Irim down with her.

Carefully, now. They couldn't afford a bad fall, or Irim wouldn't be able to get back up.

"Let's slow down," Pelisma said. "Don't lose your balance trying to guide me; talk me through. Tell me what obstacles you see."

"All right."

She reined herself to a creep, testing with her feet as though navigating a limestone tunnel with an uncertain floor. Irim's instructions were halting, and he often paused for words, but they were a way to navigate the uncertain dark. Slowly, so slowly, light grew around them.

"Almost there," Irim panted. "There's a big fallen tree. Let me rest a second; we'll have to climb over."

They leaned against it for a moment. Its bark was rough, covered with ticklish moss. When Pelisma regained her breath, she felt her way over it. A wind came rushing through the forest, bringing with it the distinct wickering sound of wings. This time it also brought the breath of warmth that promised the presence of a shinca tree.

No sooner had she reached the other side than there was a sharp pain on her left wrist. She slapped her hand to it, and discovered the prickly body of a large insect between her fingers. Other tickles along her skin were suddenly explained; she tried to brush the bugs off, but they clung and bit, forcing her to crush them one by one. Heile's mercy but they could bite!

Suddenly the sound of wings came at them in a rush.

"Pelisma!" Irim cried. He reached her, seizing her arm just as the flood rushed over them. Bird bodies bumped against her, wings struck, and feathers whipped against her face.

Then they were gone.

"Are you all right?" Irim asked.

"Yes." In fact, there was a distinct improvement. "I think they've eaten those bugs."

"There are thousands of birds," Irim said. "They're all perched up in the shinca's branches." The flood of wing-sounds began again, but this time grew quieter, as if the birds had gone off in another direction. "A whole crowd of them just flew away, but more keep coming."

She could only guess from his tone that they must not look actively dangerous. "Perhaps they need the warmth also," she said. "If we stay low beside the ground, I hope they will let us be."

"I hope so, too."

Nearer the shinca, her eyes filled with formless light. The ground felt softer, flat and springy with something that might have been moss. The green scent of it heightened with every step, and the warmth drew her nearer until she touched the shinca's glass-smooth trunk. Marvelous, marvelous heat! She set her back against it and sank down onto the moss.

Ahhhh!

For an instant, nothing existed in the world except heat, light, and the life pounding back into her frozen limbs.

"Pelisma!" Irim cried.

She shook herself, and tried to shove the feeling away—but the warmth was too wonderful to ignore. "Irim, are you all right?"

"A wysp," he stammered. "A wysp—it came so close, and it was so big—it was full of fire!"

"But it's been hours since *our* fire . . . " Could it have been following her all this time? The thought made her shudder.

An explosion of wings burst from the shinca crown above, drawing an invisible arc in the forest air before them. Amidst it came a feral growl, and then a shriek, before the arc completed its circle behind their head.

Pelisma pressed her back harder against the shinca. Now was not the time to lose touch with reality. "Irim, something is hunting the birds."

"Cave-cat," Irim muttered. "I can't see it clearly, but I doubt one bird will satisfy its appetite. We're not safe here."

"How can we move? At least here, we have the shinca at our backs." A cave-cat was definitely fierce enough to overpower one old woman and one half-broken man. The only mercy was that it was tangible.

What could anyone do against an *intangible* predator?

How small we are here! Lost, surrounded by wilderness, cut off from all human help, and that cave-cat could pounce any second—we'll be erased—

The lonely fear spiked, overwhelming her.

"Get!" Irim snapped. "Get away!"

She shook her head. "What—?"

"Wysp," said Irim grimly. "Same one I saw before—it's bigger than my hand. Look, as far as the cave-cat goes, we'll be all right. The weapon I brought is still in my pocket. But for the wysp I'm not so sure."

"A weapon?" That turned her stomach. "Irim, that's dangerous!"

"What choice do I have?"

"Cave-cat or no, an energy-thrower will only make the wysps more deadly." She cast about for something to give him pause. "What if they're souls I failed to save in the Trao flood, and they're following me to take revenge?"

Irim grunted. "I think you'd be dead already."

She couldn't argue with that. "Still, what if you miss the cat, and set the forest on fire instead? Our miraculous escape from the crash will be for nothing."

"Groundbreaker—I'm not sure we've escaped at all."

So he sensed it, too. She shivered despite the heat at her back. "Why?"

"That giant wysp is still here. Hovering, like it's waiting for us to join it." He grunted in pain. "And see? The cave-cat is back . . . "

In her mind, the wysp seemed to be Mother Elinda's herald, announcing her intent to take their spirits into her peace-giving arms. Would she bear them upward to the heavens, or would they remain here to haunt their own city for eternity?

I'm not ready to die!

In defiance of the vision, she asked, "Can you tell me what it looks like?"

"What *what* looks like? The cat?"

"The wysp."

"Why do you care what it looks like?!"

He sounded near panic. She reached out and found his arm—unfortunately, not the one with the weapon. "Irim, give me the weapon. Please."

"I should just shoot now. The cat's close enough."

She tightened her grip on his arm. "The wysps will kill you if you miss."

"Hey, I know!" he cried suddenly. "I'll shoot the wysp!"

"You're not serious—"

"I am. It's big enough to hit, and whatever discharge it creates should also scare the cat away."

"Don't."

"Groundbreaker, you know all about taking risks to defy the odds. When the river came into Pelismara, you stopped it with the most incredible explosion anyone had ever seen! Besides, I'd happily give my life to save yours."

He must still be concussed, not thinking clearly; if the wysp survived the hit, it might easily kill them both. *Will it be fire that destroys me? Or teeth and claws?* No, she had to keep her head, not give in to fear . . . . "Irim, please, humor a blind woman. Just tell me what the wysp looks like."

Irim gave an exasperated sigh. "It looks like—I guess, like a tangled ball of spider-silk set on fire."

The image blossomed unexpectedly in her head, a gorgeous conspiracy of memory and imagination. "Beautiful," she murmured, and in an instant the feeling exploded out of her control.

Great heavens, what I would give to see it, really to see this beautiful, warm, miraculous thing!

The weird desire was so strong it brought tears to her eyes, and throbbed within her like ripples nudging against a riverbank. Was her mind finally crumbling?

"No," Irim cried. "Get away, you!"

The wysp—it was still here. It was so brilliantly clear in her imagination, and the desire so strong, it seemed larger than she was. *Let me see it . . . see it . . .*

"Irim," she murmured, "Do *you* feel anything?"

Irim's voice tightened. "Pelisma, move away!"

Thinking was becoming difficult; moving, impossible. "No."

"But it's too close to you—I can't shoot it!"

She shook her head. "Irim, don't try. Don't worry about me. Protect yourself—you're young, accomplished, and I'm just an old woman who can't even see a wysp . . . "

Let me see it . . . see it . . .

His voice quivered. "But I have to save you. You're the hero of our city."

If only she could wrest the weapon from his hand! "Irim," she pleaded. "I didn't save Pelismara with dynamite and explosions. I saved it by creating an *outlet*. By letting the river flow through."

Let me see it, oh please, let me see it . . .

Wait. *Flow through?* She could feel her control eroding in the flood. If she just let go, would the surge pass by and become manageable?

Or would she lose her sanity forever? She wouldn't surrender without praying for one last bargain.

O Wanderer, I'm ready to give myself up; only help poor frightened Irim home.

She stopped fighting.

Searing heat stabbed into her head and spread outward in a shock wave of agony. Faintly, she heard herself scream.

Everything was lost in light.

Pelisma opened her eyes.

Glory blazed above her. A shinca crown: one perfect crystalline column dividing in two, then in two, then in two again and again, a glowing fractal tree transforming into a cloud of needlepoints against a solid black sky.

I'm dead.

But she could still feel her body. If anything, her blood felt, not cold, but too warm. It hummed, and there was more of it than there should have been, filling her to the brim. Maybe that wasn't her blood at all.

"Breathe," Irim's voice begged. "Don't leave me, Pelisma, breathe!"

She drew a breath, surprised it had anywhere to enter, with her so full. She couldn't look away from the perfect clarity of the shinca crown. If she moved, surely this apparition would vanish, shrouded again by the vague shadows of her vision.

She whispered, "Irim . . . ?"

"Thank Heile!" he exclaimed. "When that wysp flew through you, I thought you were dead for sure. But it's gone now."

"It . . . " Her voice sounded normal enough, but words came slowly. "It flowed through?" The pain was gone, and the strange desire too, but a feeling of presence remained. Had that emotional deluge not been her own at all? Had it been the wysp manipulating her?

How delightful!

But it wasn't, it wasn't! It shouldn't be possible to feel anything resembling innocent excitement in such circumstances!

Unless the feeling wasn't her own.

"Irim, the wysp flowed in," Pelisma said. "I don't think it flowed out again. It's still here."

"Heile have mercy," Irim said. "Has the spirit spoken to you?"

"Spoken!" she cried. "It doesn't *speak* at all!" Icy panic shot down her nerves, but melted inexplicably before it could reach her fingertips. Suddenly she wanted nothing more than to hold someone and apologize. She hugged herself, looked down instinctively—

And saw a glowing golden shape against the black.

Was this her imagination? It couldn't be sight—but the shape was that of her own body. Her clothes, her fingernails, even the wrinkles on her knuckles, all lay like a tracery of dark lace over a golden glow within. She held her hands up, considering the folds of her palms for the first time in months, hardly daring to blink. If it wasn't sight, then what was it?

"Pelisma, what's going on?" Irim asked.

She could hardly speak. "Irim—Irim, I can *see*. Do wysps see? Well, I suppose they must." *This* excitement was real! She looked around.

It was not the forest of her memory, glowing with green. It was not the black of night, nor yet the vague mass of shadow usually detected by her failing eyes. The wilderness had changed: now it was rendered in finely detailed layers of transparency, as if built entirely of smoky crystal. It had scents, too, in a strange organization she could scarcely comprehend. Shinca stood out even from great distance, each raising a blazing crystalline crown toward the dark sky, around which wysps swirled in complex patterns. Beneath her feet, soil and rock rippled outward like deep, clear water.

This was not a human world. And it was no longer cold, except to Irim. Irim, who was wounded and needed rescue.

"Irim," she said, "stay by the tree. I'm going back to the waymarkers."

"Pelisma, you can't! That cave-cat's still out there."

He was right, of course. She searched the strange landscape, but how could she identify a cave-cat in this new sense, among twenty thousand utterly unfamiliar things? "Do you see the cat?" she asked. "Can you show me where it is, so I can figure out what it looks like?"

"What it *looks like*?" Irim took a deep breath and grasped her hand firmly. "Groundbreaker, it's my job to protect you. Eyesight like yours does not get cured—certainly not in an instant. We have no idea what that wysp did to you, or why."

"I'm not cured," she said. "I understand that. It's not exactly *seeing*, anyway. Irim—" She squeezed his hand. "I'm not sure how to tell you this, but the wysp—it's not human."

"It might be a quiet soul—"

"It can't be. Not unless there are folk who see through stone, for whom shinca and wysps are more real than people."

"Is that what you see?" He was silent a moment. "But they must be spirits of *some* kind. Where else would they all come from?"

Where else, indeed? She sought for wysps in the shinca crown above her head, and as if she'd called them, several immediately converged on her position.

Irim gave a hoarse cry and fired his weapon.

Zzap!

Fire exploded from the shadows, a voracious living nightmare screaming alarms down every nerve in her body.

It felt like the river pouring in at the gate, faster every second. If she didn't act, it would consume everything she cared about, every living thing! Pelisma leapt toward the flames, opened her mouth—

And swallowed them.

Energy blazed inside her, buzzing to the tips of her fingers and toes, tingling in her lips, and it was full of outrage for those who would put her world at risk. She whirled, looking past the bright silver-gold column of the shinca, and found a fainter light, the imprint of accumulated heat scented with fear and anger. Out of that imprint came a quavering voice.

"Pelisma?"

Pelisma opened her mouth to answer, but the energy within her rose in a sudden, terrifying tide. In an instant, she realized what it meant.

No! Not Irim, I mustn't hurt Irim!

She turned, barely in time. White flame poured from her mouth, crackling in the air.

Irim screamed.

She tried to stop, but there was no containing this flood. Horrified, she turned further; the edge of the torrent touched the shinca, and somehow, vanished into it.

That's it.

She faced the tree fully, pouring this hate out in the one place where it could do no harm. Anger surged in her heart, but she fought against it.

No, you don't understand! Poor Irim, poor fellow, he didn't mean it, he doesn't deserve to die!

At last the fire drained away. She fell against the shinca, shivering. Slowly, her horrified exhaustion softened with an incongruous feeling of comfort and regret.

"Irim?" she asked, trembling. "In the name of Heile, tell me I haven't killed you . . . "

"Stay away from me!"

Pelisma fell to her knees. Tears tumbled from her eyes. "Irim, it was an accident, I promise. It won't happen again."

Voices called across the forest.

She raised her head. "Help!" she shouted. "Please, help us!"

The searchers came. They wrapped her in blankets, brought a stretcher for Irim. She could see its metal struts perfectly; also, the waymarkers and the vehicle that stood waiting.

"It's lucky you found a way to signal us," the driver rumbled. "Otherwise we might not have found you for hours."

"Lucky indeed," agreed the medic. The faint shadows that were her hands moved swiftly and busily over Irim. "The Wanderer must have been watching over you."

"Thanks be," Pelisma agreed, and found Irim echoing her precisely.

"You'll be safe underground soon."

"Thank you," Pelisma said.

They would be safe, wouldn't they? How could she be sure, when the wysp might control her actions? She touched Irim's shoulder, and her sick guilt was diluted with another incongruous feeling of tender and sorrowful care.

She hadn't killed him, though. She had to remember that. When the wysp took over, she'd managed to communicate mercy.

To communicate.

A pattern clicked into place, suddenly.

Her blindness had brought feelings of sorrow and helplessness, but the serious emotional instability had begun with the presence of wysps. Since she'd hidden her feelings from Irim, there would have been no way to link them with the moment of a wysp's approach—but here in the forest, her feelings had resisted control *every time wysps were nearby.*

What if these incongruous emotions weren't weakness, or age, but communication?

Imagine what it could mean to achieve real communication with this thing that was the most capricious, dangerous force in all Varin! A question leapt into her mind, full of unfiltered, helpless anger.

Why, wysp? Why did you turn me against my most trusted friend?

For an instant she found herself back in that moment, when the fire of Irim's weapon had mixed with her memory of the Trao thundering in at the gate. The familiar awful conviction rose within her, that if she did not act, her world would be swept away.

Not her world: *their* world.

Perhaps wysps did have souls: souls suited to this wilderness as her own people were to the city-caverns, each just as easily threatened, but with no way to communicate until disaster threw them together.

Oh, praise be!

Was this joy hers, or did it belong to both of them? Could she ever untangle the wysp's meanings enough to answer questions about fire, and trees, and food grown beneath the sun—those questions her people so desperately needed to have answered?

All at once, she remembered Irim's voice, reading reverently. *Great things may be achieved in the name of love.*

"Blessing of Eyn," Pelisma breathed. Surely the Wanderer had brought her to these events. Blindness had turned her people's confinement into her own, changing her heart and bringing the wysps—her people's threat turned into a personal need. What else could have driven her out into this voyage of discovery? And now her path was clear: she must learn everything possible about the wysps, their vision, and their world.

Think how she might then change her own.

ABOUT THE AUTHOR

Juliette Wade has turned her studies in linguistics, anthropology and Japanese language and culture into tools for writing fantasy and science fiction. She lives the Bay Area of Northern California with her husband and two children, who support and inspire her. She blogs about language and culture in SF/F at TalkToYoUniverse and runs the "Dive into Worldbuilding!" hangout series on Google+. Her fiction has appeared several times in *Analog Science Fiction and Fact,* and in various anthologies.

The Halfway House
at the Heart of Darkness
WILLIAM BROWNING SPENCER

Keel wore a ragged shirt with the holo Veed There, Simmed That shimmering on it. She wore it in and out of the virtual. If she was in an interactive virtual, the other players sometimes complained. Amid the dragons and elves and swords of fire, a bramble-haired girl, obviously spiking her virtual with drugs and refusing to tune her shirt to something suitably medieval, could be distracting.

"Fizz off," Keel would say, in response to all complaints.

Keel was difficult. Rich, self-destructive, beautiful, she was twenty years old and already a case study in virtual psychosis.

She had been rehabbed six times. She could have died that time on Makor when she went blank in the desert. She still bore the teeth marks of the land eels that were gnawing on her shoulder when they found her.

A close one. You can't revive the digested.

No one had to tell Keel that she was in rehab again. She was staring at a green ocean, huge white clouds overhead, white gulls filling the heated air with their cries.

They gave you these serenity mock-ups when they were bringing you around. They were fairly insipid and several shouts behind the technology. This particular V-run was embarrassing. The ocean wasn't continuous, probably a seven-minute repeat, and the sun's heat was patchy on her face.

The beach was empty. She was propped up in a lounge chair—no doubt her position back in the ward. With concentration, focusing on her spine, she could sense the actual contours of the bed, the satiny feel of the sensor pad.

It was work, this focusing, and she let it go. Always better to flow.

Far to her right, she spied a solitary figure. The figure was moving toward her.

It was, she knew, a wilson. She was familiar with the drill. Don't spook the patient. Approach her slowly after she is sedated and in a quiet setting.

The wilson was a fat man in a white suit (*neo-Victorian, dead silly,* Keel thought). He kept his panama hat from taking flight in the wind by clamping it onto his head with his right hand and leaning forward.

Keel recognized him. She even remembered his name, but then It was the kind of name you'd remember: Dr. Max Marx.

He had been her counselor, her wilson, the last time she'd crashed. Which meant she was in Addiction Resources Limited, which was located just outside of New Vegas.

Dr. Marx looked up, waved, and came on again with new purpose.

A pool of sadness welled in her throat. There was nothing like help, and its pale sister hope, to fill Keel's soul with black water.

Fortunately, Dr. Max Marx wasn't one of the hearty ones. The hearty ones were the worst. Marx was, in fact, refreshingly gloomy, his thick black beard and eyebrows creating a doomed stoic's countenance.

"Yes," he said, in response to her criticism of the virtual, "this is a very miserable effect. You should see the sand crabs. They are laughable, like toys." He eased himself down on the sand next to her and took his hat off and fanned it in front of his face. "I apologize. It must be very painful, a connoisseur of the vee like you, to endure this."

Keel remembered that Dr. Marx spoke in a manner subject to interpretation. His words always held a potential for sarcasm.

"We are portable," Dr. Marx said. "We are in a mobile unit, and so, alas, we don't have the powerful stationary AdRes equipment at our command. Even so, we could do better, there are better mock-ups to be had, but we are not prospering these days. Financially, it has been a year of setbacks, and we have had to settle for some second-rate stuff."

"I'm not in a hospital?" Keel asked.

Marx shook his head. "No. No hospital."

Keel frowned. Marx, sensing her confusion, put his hat back on his head and studied her through narrowed eyes. "We are on the run, Keel Benning. You have not been following the news, being otherwise occupied, but companies like your beloved Virtvana have won a major legislative battle. They are now empowered to maintain their customer base aggressively. I believe the wording is 'protecting customer assets against invasive alienation by third-party services.' Virtvana can come and get you."

Keel blinked at Dr. Marx's dark countenance. "You can't seriously think someone would . . . what? . . . kidnap me?"

Dr. Marx shrugged. "Virtvana might. For the precedent. You're a good customer."

"Vee moguls are going to sweat the loss of one spike? That's crazy."

Dr. Marx sighed, stood up, whacked sand from his trousers with his hands. "You noticed then? That's good. Being able to recognize crazy, that is a good sign. It means there is hope for your own sanity."

Her days were spent at the edge of the second-rate ocean. She longed for something that would silence the Need. She would have settled for a primitive bird-in-flight simulation. Anything. Some corny sex-with-dolphins loop—or something abstract, the color red leaking into blue, enhanced with aural-D.

She would have given ten years of her life for a game of Apes and Angels, Virtvana's most popular package. Apes and Angels wasn't just another smooth metaphysical mix—it was the true religion to its fans. A gamer started out down in the muck on Libido Island, where the senses were indulged with perfect, shimmerless sims. Not bad, Libido Island, and some gamers stayed there a long, long time. But what put Apes and Angels above the best pleasure pops was this: A player could *evolve spiritually.* If you followed the Path, if you were steadfast, you became more compassionate, more aware, at one with the universe . . . all of which was accompanied by feelings of euphoria.

Keel would have settled for a legal rig. Apes and Angels was a chemically enhanced virtual, and the gear that true believers wore was stripped of most safeguards, tuned to a higher reality.

It was one of these hot pads that had landed Keel in Addiction Resources again.

"It's the street stuff that gets you in trouble," Keel said. "I've just got to stay clear of that."

"You said that last time," the wilson said. "You almost died, you know."

Keel felt suddenly hollowed, beaten. "Maybe I want to die," she said.

Dr. Marx shrugged. Several translucent seagulls appeared, hovered over him, and then winked out. "Bah," he muttered. "Bad therapy-V, bad, death-wishing clients, bad career choice. Who doesn't want to die? And who doesn't get that wish, sooner or later?"

• • •

One day, Dr. Marx said, "You are ready for swimming."

It was morning, full of a phony, golden light. The nights were black and dreamless, nothing, and the days that grew out of them were pale and untaxing. It was an intentionally bland virtual, its sameness designed for healing.

Keel was wearing a one-piece, white bathing suit. Her counselor wore bathing trunks, baggy with thick black vertical stripes; he looked particularly solemn, in an effort, no doubt, to counteract the farcical elements of rotund belly and sticklike legs.

Keel sighed. She knew better than to protest. This was necessary. She took her wilson's proffered hand, and they walked down to the water's edge. The sand changed from white to gray where the water rolled over it, and they stepped forward into the salt-smelling foam.

Her legs felt cold when the water enclosed them. The wetness was now more than virtual. As she leaned forward and kicked, her muscles, taut and frayed, howled.

She knew the machines were exercising her now. Somewhere her real body, emaciated from long neglect, was swimming in a six-foot aquarium whose heavy seas circulated to create a kind of liquid treadmill. Her lungs ached; her shoulders twisted into monstrous knots of pain.

In the evening, they would talk, sitting in their chairs and watching the ocean swallow the sun, the clouds turning orange, the sky occasionally spotting badly, some sort of pixel fatigue.

"If human beings are the universe's way of looking at itself," Dr. Marx said, "then virtual reality is the universe's way of pretending to look at itself."

"You wilsons are all so down on virtual reality," Keel said. "But maybe it is the natural evolution of perception. I mean, everything we see is a product of the equipment we see it with. Biological, mechanical, whatever."

Dr. Marx snorted. "Bah. The old 'everything-is-virtual' argument. I am ashamed of you, Keel Benning. Something more original, please. We wilsons are down on virtual addiction because everywhere we look we see dead philosophers. We see them and they don't look so good. We smell them, and they stink. That is our perception, our primitive reality."

The healing was slow, and the sameness, the boredom, was a hole to be filled with words. Keel talked, again, about the death of her parents and her brother. They had been over this ground the last time she'd been in treatment, but she was here again, and so it was said again.

"I'm rich because they are dead," she said.

It was true, of course, and Dr. Marx merely nodded, staring in front of him. Her father had been a wealthy man, and he and his young wife and Keel's brother, Calder, had died in a freak air-docking accident while vacationing at Keypond Terraforms. A "sole survivor" clause in her father's life insurance policy had left Keel a vast sum.

She had been eleven at the time—and would have died with her family had she not been sulking that day, refusing to leave the hotel suite.

She knew she was not responsible, of course. But it was not an event you wished to dwell on. You looked, naturally, for powerful distractions.

"It is a good excuse for your addiction," Dr. Marx said. "If you die, maybe God will say, 'I don't blame you.' Or maybe God will say, 'Get real. Life's hard.' I don't know. Addiction is in the present, not the past. It's the addiction itself that leads to more addictive behavior."

Keel had heard all this before. She barely heard it this time. The weariness of the evening was real, brought on by the day's physical exertions. She spoke in a kind of woozy, presleep fog, finding no power in her words, no emotional release.

Of more interest were her counselor's words. He spoke with rare candor, the result, perhaps, of their fugitive status, their isolation.

It was after a long silence that he said, "To tell you the truth, I'm thinking of getting out of the addiction treatment business. I'm sick of being on the losing side."

Keel felt a coldness in her then, which, later, she identified as fear.

He continued: "They are winning. Virtvana, MindSlide, Right to Flight. They've got the sex, the style, and the flash. All we wilsons have is a sense of mission, this knowledge that people are dying, and the ones that don't die are being lost to lives of purpose.

"Maybe we're right—sure, we're right—but we can't sell it. In two, three days we'll come to our destination and you'll have to come into Big R and meet your fellow addicts. You won't be impressed. It's a henry-hovel in the Slash. It's not a terrific advertisement for Big R."

Keel felt strange, comforting her wilson. Nonetheless, she reached forward and touched his bare shoulder. "You want to help people. That is a good and noble impulse."

He looked up at her, a curious nakedness in his eyes. "Maybe that is hubris.

"Hubris?"

"Are you not familiar with the word? It means to try to steal the work of the gods."

Keel thought about that in the brief moment between the dimming of the seascape and the nothingness of night. She thought it would be a fine thing to do, to steal the work of the gods.

Dr. Marx checked the perimeter, the security net. All seemed to be in order. The air was heavy with moisture and the cloying odor of mint. This mint scent was the olfactory love song of an insect-like creature that flourished in the tropical belt. The creature looked like an unpleasant mix of spider and wasp. Knowing that the sweet scent came from it, Dr. Marx breathed shallowly and had to fight against an inclination to gag. Interesting, the way knowledge affected one. An odor, pleasant in itself, could induce nausea when its source was identified.

He was too weary to pursue the thought. He returned to the mobile unit, climbed in and locked the door behind him. He walked down the corridor, paused to peer into the room where Keel rested, sedated electrically.

He should not have spoken his doubts. He was weary, depressed, and it was true that he might very well abandon this crumbling profession. But he had no right to be so self-revealing to a client. As long as he was employed, it behooved him to conduct himself in a professional manner.

Keel's head rested quietly on the pillow. Behind her, on the green panels, her heart and lungs created cool, luminous graphics. Physically, she was restored. Emotionally, mentally, spiritually, she might be damaged beyond repair.

He turned away from the window and walked on down the corridor. He walked past his sleeping quarters to the control room. He undressed and lay down on the utilitarian flat and let the neuronet embrace him. He was aware, as always, of guilt and a hangdog sense of betrayal.

The virtual had come on the Highway two weeks ago. He'd already left Addiction Resources with Keel, traveling west into the wilderness of Pit Finitum, away from the treatment center and New Vegas.

Know the enemy. He'd sampled all the vees, played at lowest res with all the safeguards maxed, so that he could talk knowledgeably with his clients. But he'd never heard of this virtual—and it had a special fascination for him. It was called *Halfway House.*

A training vee, not a recreational one, it consisted of a series of step-motivated, instructional virtuals designed to teach the apprentice addictions counselor his trade.

So why this guilt attached to methodically running the course?

What guilt?

That guilt.

Okay. Well . . .

The answer was simple enough: Here all interventions came to a good end, all problems were resolved, all clients were healed.

So far he had intervened on a fourteen-year-old boy addicted to Clawhammer Comix, masterfully diagnosed a woman suffering from Leary's syndrome, and led an entire group of mix-feeders through a nasty withdrawal episode.

He could tell himself he was learning valuable healing techniques.

Or he could tell himself that he was succumbing to the world that killed his clients, the hurt-free world where everything worked out for the best, good triumphed, bad withered and died, rewards came effortlessly—and if that was not enough, the volume could always be turned up.

He had reservations. Adjusting the neuronet, he thought, "I will be careful." It was what his clients always said.

Keel watched the insipid ocean, waited. Generally, Dr. Marx arrived soon after the darkness of sleep had fled.   He did not come at all. When the sun was high in the sky, she began to shout for him. That was useless, of course.

She ran into the ocean, but it was a low res ghost and only filled her with vee-panic. She stumbled back to the beach chair, tried to calm herself with a rational voice: *Someone will come.*

But would they? She was, according to her wilson, in the wilds of Pit Finitum, hundreds of miles to the west of New Vegas, traveling toward a halfway house hidden in some dirty corner of the mining warren known as the Slash.

Darkness came, and the programmed current took her into unconsciousness.

The second day was the same, although she sensed a physical weakness that emanated from Big R. Probably nutrients in one of the IV pockets had been depleted. *I'll die,* she thought. Night snuffed the thought.

A new dawn arrived without Dr. Marx. Was he dead? And if so, was he dead by accident or design? And if by design, whose? Perhaps he had killed himself; perhaps this whole business of Virtvana's persecution was a delusion.

Keel remembered the wilson's despair, felt a sudden conviction that Dr. Marx had fled Addiction Resources without that center's knowledge, a victim of the evangelism/paranoia psychosis that sometimes accompanied counselor burnout.

Keel had survived much in her twenty years. She had donned some deadly v-gear and made it back to Big R intact. True, she had been saved a couple of times, and she probably wasn't what anyone would call psychologically sound, but . . . it would be an ugly irony if it was an addictions rehab, an unhinged wilson, that finally killed her.

Keel hated irony, and it was this disgust that pressed her into action.

She went looking for the plug. She began by focusing on her spine, the patches, the slightly off-body temp of the sensor pad. Had her v-universe been more engrossing, this would have been harder to do, but the ocean was deteriorating daily, the seagulls now no more than scissoring disruptions in the mottled sky.

On the third afternoon of her imposed solitude, she was able to sit upright in Big R. It required all her strength, the double-think of real Big-R motion while in the virtual. The affect in vee was to momentarily tilt the ocean and cause the sky to leak blue pixels into the sand.

Had her arms been locked, had her body been glove-secured, it would have been wasted effort, of course, but Keel's willing participation in her treatment, her daily exercise regimen, had allowed relaxed physical inhibitors. There had been no reason for Dr. Marx to anticipate Keel's attempting a Big-R disruption.

She certainly didn't want to.

The nausea and terror induced by contrary motion in Big R while simulating a virtual was considerable.

Keel relied on gravity, shifting, leaning to the right. The bed shifted to regain balance.

She screamed, twisted, hurled herself sideways into Big R.

And her world exploded. The ocean raced up the beach, a black tidal wave that screeched and rattled as though some monstrous mechanical beast were being demolished by giant pistons.

Black water engulfed her. She coughed and it filled her lungs. She flayed; her right fist slammed painfully against the side of the container, making it hum.

She clambered out of the exercise vat, placed conveniently next to the bed, stumbled, and sprawled on the floor in naked triumph.

"Hello Big R," she said, tasting blood on her lips.

Dr. Marx had let the system ease him back into Big R. The sessions room dimmed to glittering black, then the light returned. He was back in the bright control room. He removed the neuronet, swung his legs to the side of the flatbed, stretched. It had been a good session. He had learned something about distinguishing (behaviorally) the transitory feedback psychosis called frets from the organic v-disease, Viller's Pathway.

This Halfway House was proving to be a remarkable instructional tool. In retrospect, his fear of its virtual form had been pure superstition. He smiled at his own irrationality.

He would have slept that night in ignorance, but he decided to give the perimeter of his makeshift compound a last security check before retiring.

To that effect, he dressed and went outside.

In the flare of the compound lights, the jungle's purple vegetation looked particularly unpleasant, like the swollen limbs of long-drowned corpses. The usual skittering things made a racket. There was nothing in the area inclined to attack a man, but the planet's evolution hadn't stinted on biting and stinging vermin, and . . .

And one of the vermin was missing.

He had, as always, been frugal in his breathing, gathering into his lungs as little of the noxious atmosphere as possible. The cloying mint scent never failed to sicken him.

But the odor was gone.

It had been there earlier in the evening, and now it was gone. He stood in jungle night, in the glare of the compound lights, waiting for his brain to process this piece of information, but his brain told him only that the odor had been there and now it was gone.

Still, some knowledge of what this meant was leaking through, creating a roiling fear.

If you knew what to look for, you could find it. No vee was as detailed as nature.

You only had to find one seam, one faint oscillation in a rock, one incongruent shadow.

It was a first-rate sim, and it would have fooled him. But they had had to work fast, fabricating and downloading it, and no one had noted that a nasty alien bug filled the Big-R air with its mating fragrance.

Dr. Marx knew he was still in the vee. That meant, of course, that he had not walked outside at all. He was still lying on the flat. And, thanks to his blessed paranoia, there was a button at the base of the flat, two inches from where his left hand naturally lay. Pushing it would disrupt all current and activate a hypodermic containing twenty cc's of hapotile-4. Hapotile-4 could get the attention of the deepest v-diver. The aftereffects were not pleasant, but, for many v-devotees, there wouldn't have been an "after" without hapotile.

Dr. Marx didn't hesitate. He strained for the Big R, traced the line of his arm, moved. It was there; he found it. Pressed.

Nothing.

Then, out of the jungle, a figure came.

Eight feet tall, carved from black steel, the vee soldier bowed at the waist. Then, standing erect, it spoke: "We deactivated your failsafe before you embarked, Doctor."

"Who are you?" He was not intimidated by this military mockup, the boom of its metal voice, the faint whine of its servos. It was a virtual puppet, of course. Its masters were the thing to fear.

"We are concerned citizens," the soldier said. "We have reason to believe that you are preventing a client of ours, a client-in-good-credit, from satisfying her constitutionally sanctioned appetites."

"Keel Benning came to us of her own free will. Ask her and she will tell you as much."

"We will ask her. And that is not what she will say. She will say, for all the world to hear, that her freedom was compromised by so-called caregivers."

"Leave her alone."

The soldier came closer. It looked up at the dark blanket of the sky. "Too late to leave anyone alone, Doctor. Everyone is in the path of progress. One day we will all live in the vee. It is the natural home of gods."

The sky began to glow as the black giant raised its gleaming arms.

"You act largely out of ignorance," the soldier said. "The godseekers come, and you treat them like aberrations, like madmen burning with sickness. This is because you do not know the virtual yourself. Fearing it, you have confined and studied it. You have refused to taste it, to savor it."

The sky was glowing gold, and figures seemed to move in it, beautiful, winged humanforms.

Virtvana, Marx thought. *Apes and Angels.*

It was his last coherent thought before enlightenment.

"I give you a feast," the soldier roared. And all the denizens of heaven swarmed down, surrounding Dr. Marx with love and compassion and that absolute, impossible distillation of a hundred thousand insights that formed a single, tear-shaped truth: Euphoria.

Keel found she could stand. A couple of days of inaction hadn't entirely destroyed the work of all that exercise. Shakily, she navigated the small room. The room had the sanitized, hospital look she'd grown to know and loathe. If this room followed the general scheme, the shelves over the bed should contain . . . They did, and Keel donned one of the gray, disposable client suits.

She found Dr. Marx by the noise he was making, a kind of huh, huh, huh delivered in a monotonous chant and punctuated by an occasional Ah! The sounds, and the writhing, near-naked body that lay on the table emitting these sounds, suggested to Keel that her doctor, naughty man, might be auditing something sexual on the virtual.

But a closer look showed signs of v-overload epilepsy. Keel had seen it before and knew that one's first inclination, to shut down every incoming signal, was not the way to go. First you shut down any chemical enhancers—and, if you happened to have a hospital handy (as she did), you slowed the system more with something like clemadine or hetlin—then, if you were truly fortunate and your spike was epping in a high-tech detox (again, she was so fortunate), you plugged in a regulator, spliced it and started running the signals through that, toning them down.

Keel got to it. As she moved, quickly, confidently, she had time to think that this was something she knew about (a consumer's knowledge, not a tech's, but still, her knowledge was extensive).

Dr. Marx had been freed from the virtual for approximately ten minutes (but was obviously not about to break the surface of Big R), when Keel heard the whine of the security alarm. The front door of the unit was being breached with an L-saw.

Keel scrambled to the corridor where she'd seen the habitat sweep. She swung the ungainly tool around, falling to one knee as she struggled to unbolt the barrel lock. *Fizzing pocky low-tech grubber.*

The barrel-locking casing clattered to the floor just as the door collapsed.

The man in the doorway held a weapon, which, in retrospect, made Keel feel a little better. Had he been weaponless, she would still have done what she did.

She swept him out the door. The sonic blast scattered him across the cleared area, a tumbling, bloody mass of rags and unraveling flesh, a thigh bone tumbling into smaller bits as it rolled under frayed vegetation.

She was standing in the doorway when an explosion rocked the unit and sent her crashing backward. She crawled down the corridor, still lugging the habitat gun, and fell into the doorway of a cluttered storage room. An alarm continued to shriek somewhere.

The mobile now lay on its side. She fired in front of her. The roof rippled and roared, looked like it might hold, and then flapped away like an unholy, howling v-demon, a vast silver blade that smoothly severed the leafy tops of the jungle's tallest sentinels. Keel plunged into the night, ran to the edge of the unit and peered out into the glare of the compound lights.

The man was crossing the clearing.

She crouched, and he turned, sensing motion. He was trained to fire reflexively but he was too late. The rolling sonic blast from Keel's habitat gun swept man and weapon and weapon's discharge into roiling motes that mixed with rock and sand and vegetation, a stew of organic and inorganic matter for the wind to stir.

Keel waited for others to come but none did.

Finally, she reentered the mobile to retrieve her wilson, dragging him (unconscious) into the scuffed arena of the compound.

Later that night, exhausted, she discovered the aircraft that had brought the two men. She hesitated, then decided to destroy it. It would do her no good; it was not a vehicle she could operate, and its continued existence might bring others.

The next morning, Keel's mood improved when she found a pair of boots that almost fit. They were a little tight but, she reasoned, that was probably better than a little loose. They had, according to Dr. Marx, a four-day trek ahead of them.

Dr. Marx was now conscious but fairly insufferable. He could talk about nothing but angels and the Light. A long, hard dose of Apes and Angels had filled him with fuzzy love and an uncomplicated metaphysics in which smiling angels fixed bad stuff and protected all good people (and, it went without saying, all people were good).

Keel had managed to dress Dr. Marx in a suit again, and this restored a professional appearance to the wilson. But, to Keel's dismay, Dr. Marx in virtual-withdrawal was a shameless whiner.

"Please," he would implore. "Please, I am in terrible terrible Neeeeeeed."

He complained that the therapy-v was too weak, that he was sinking into a catatonic state. Later, he would stop entirely, of course, but now, please, something stronger . . . .

No.

He told her she was heartless, cruel, sadistic, vengeful. She was taking revenge for her own treatment program, although, if she would just recall, he had been the soul of gentleness and solicitude.

"You can't be in virtual and make the journey," Keel said. "I need you to navigate. We will take breaks, but I'm afraid they will brief. Say goodbye to your mobile."

She destroyed it with the habitat sweep, and they were on their way. It was a limping, difficult progress, for they took much with them: food, emergency camping and sleeping gear, a portable, two-feed v-rig, the virtual black box, and the security image grabs. And Dr. Marx was not a good traveler.

It took six days to get to the Slash, and then Dr. Marx said he wasn't sure just where the halfway house was.

"What?"

"I don't know. I'm disoriented."

"You'll never be a good v-addict," Keel said. "You can't lie."

"I'm not lying!" Dr. Marx snapped, goggle-eyed with feigned innocence.

Keel knew what was going on. He wanted to give her the slip and find a v-hovel where he could swap good feelings with his old angel buddies. Keel knew.

"I'm not letting you out of my sight," she said.

The Slash was a squalid mining town with every vice a disenfranchised population could buy. It had meaner toys than New Vegas, and no semblance of law.

Keel couldn't just ask around for a treatment house. You could get hurt that way.

But luck was with her. She spied the symbol of a triangle inside a circle on the side of what looked like an abandoned office. She watched a man descend a flight of stairs directly beneath the painted triangle. She followed him.

"Where are we going?" Dr. Marx said. He was still a bundle of tics from angel-deprivation.

Keel didn't answer, just dragged him along. Inside, she saw the "Easy Does It" sign and knew everything was going to be okay.

An old man saw her and waved. Incredibly, he knew her, even knew her name. "Keel," he shouted. "I'm delighted to see you."

,It's a small world, Solly."

"It's that. But you get around some too. You cover some ground, you know. I figured ground might be covering you by now."

Keel laughed. "Yeah." She reached out and touched the old man's arm. "I'm looking for a house," she said.

In Group they couldn't get over it. Dr. Max Marx was a fizzing client. This amazed everyone, but two identical twins, Sere and Shona, were so dazed by this event that they insisted on dogging the wilson's every move. They'd flank him, peering into his eyes, trying to fathom this mystery by an act of unrelenting scrutiny.

Brake Madders thought it was a narc thing and wanted to hurt Marx.

"No, he's one of us," Keel said.

And so, Keel thought, *am I.*

When Dr. Max Marx was an old man, one of his favorite occupations was to reminisce. One of his favorite topics was Keel Benning. He gave her credit for saving his life, not only in the jungles of Pit Finitum but during the rocky days that followed when he wanted to flee the halfway house and find, again, virtual nirvana.

She had recognized every denial system and thwarted it with logic. When logic was not enough, she had simply shared his sadness and pain and doubt.

"I've been there," she had said.

The young wilsons and addiction activists knew Keel Benning only as the woman who had fought Virtvana and MindSlip and the vast lobby of Right to Flight, the woman who had secured a resounding victory for addicts' rights and challenged the spurious thinking that suggested a drowning person was drowning by choice. She was a hero, but, like many heroes, she was not, to a newer generation, entirely real.

"I was preoccupied at the time," Dr. Marx would tell young listeners. "I kept making plans to slip out and find some Apes and Angels. You weren't hard pressed then—and you aren't now—to find some mind-flaming vee in the Slash. My thoughts would go that way a lot.

"So I didn't stop and think, 'Here's a woman who's been rehabbed six times; it's not likely she'll stop on the seventh. She's just endured some genuine nasty events, and she's probably feeling the need for some quality downtime.'

"What I saw was a woman who spent every waking moment working on her recovery. And when she wasn't doing mental, spiritual, or physical push-ups she was helping those around her, all us shaking, vision-hungry, fizz-headed needers.

"I didn't think, 'What the hell is this?' back then. But I thought it later. I thought it when I saw her graduate from medical school."

"When she went back and got a law degree, so she could fight the bastards who wouldn't let her practice addiction medicine properly, I thought it again. That time, I asked her. I asked her what had wrought the change."

Dr. Marx would wait as long as it took for someone to ask, "What did she say?"

"It unsettled me some," he would say, then wait again to be prompted. They'd prompt.

"'Helping people,' she'd said. She'd found it was a thing she could do, she had a gift for it. All those no-counts and dead-enders in a halfway house in the Slack. She found she could help them all."

Dr. Marx saw it then, and saw it every time after that, every time he'd seen her speaking on some monolith grid at some rally, some hearing, some whatever. Once he'd seen it, he saw it every time: that glint in her eye, the incorrigible, unsinkable addict.

"People," she had said. "What a rush."

First published in *Lord of the Fantastic: Stories in Honor of Roger Zelazny,* edited by Martin H. Greenberg, 1998.

ABOUT THE AUTHOR

William Browning Spencer was born in Washington, D.C. and now lives in Austin, Texas. His first novel, *Maybe I'll Call Anna,* was published in 1990 and won a New American Writing Award, and he has subsequently made quite a reputation for himself with quirky, eccentric, eclectic novels that dance on the borderlines between horror, fantasy, and black comedy, novels such as *Resume with Monsters, Zod Wallop,* and *Irrational Fears.* His short work has been collected in *The Return of Count Electric and Other Stories* and *The Ocean and All of Its Devices.*

Gold Mountain

CHRIS ROBERSON

Johnston Lien stood at the open door of the tram, one elbow crooked around a guardrail, her blue eyes squinting in the morning glare at the sky-piercing needle of the orbital elevator to the south. The sun was in the Cold Dew position, early in the dog-month, when the temperature began to soar and the sunlight burned brighter in the southern sky. Summer was not long off, and Lien hoped to be far from here before it came. As the tram rumbled across the city of Nine Dragons, she turned her attention back to her notes, checking the address of her last interviewee and reviewing the pertinent bits of data from their brief earlier meeting.

Lien had been in Nine Dragons for well over three months, and was eager to return home to the north. She didn't care for the climate this far south, the constant humidity of the sea air, the heat of the southern sun. Nor did she have much patience for the laconic character of Guangdong, the endless farms stretching out in every direction, the slow and simple country wisdom of the southern farmers. Lien was a daughter of Beijing, the Northern Capital, and was accustomed to the hustle of crowded city streets, of nights at the Royal Opera and afternoons in ornamental gardens, of dashing officers of the Eight Banners Army and witty court scholars in their ruby-tipped hats. Nine Dragons, and the port city of Fragrant Harbor across the bay, was filled with nothing but rustics, fishermen, district bureaucrats, and workmen. The only people of culture who came through were travelers on their way to Gold Mountain, but they passed through the city and to the base of the orbital elevator while scarcely looking left or right, and before they'd had time to draw a breath of southern air into their lungs were onboard a gondola, rising up along the electromagnetic rails of Gold Mountain, up the orbital tether of the Bridge of Heaven to the orbiting city of Diamond Summit, thirty-six thousand kilometers overhead.

Johnston Lien was a researcher with the Historical Bureau of the Ministry of Celestial Excursion, and today she'd make her final site visit and collect the last of the data needed for her project. She was part of a group of scholars and researchers given the task of compiling a complete history of the early days of space exploration, beginning with the inception of the Ministry of Celestial Excursion under the aegis of the Xuantong Emperor in the previous century, and continuing straight through to the launch of the Treasure Fleet to the red planet Fire Star, which began just weeks before. The history was to be presented to the emperor in the Northern Capital when the final ship of the Treasure Fleet, a humble water-tender christened Night Shining White, departed on its months' long voyage to the red planet.

The tram approached the eastern quarter of Nine Dragons, where the buildings of Ghost Town huddled together over cramped streets, before the city gave way to docklands, and then to the open sea. Lien returned her notes and disposable brush to her satchel, and chanced a slight smile. She'd already made initial contact with this, her final interview subject, and once she'd finished with him, her work would be complete. She could return straight away to the Inn of the White Lotus, pack up her things, and board a Cloud Flyer back to the Northern Capital. Once she'd filed her findings with the chief of her bureau, she'd be able to return to her regular duties—and more, she'd be able to return to her own life.

The tram reached the easternmost point of its circuit, the driver ringing a bell to announce the last stop. Lien released her hold on the guardrail and hopped to the cobbled street, a few sad-faced old white men making their careful way down the tram's steps behind her. As the tram reversed course and made its way back toward the west, Lien walked up the narrow street, under an archway crested by a massive carved eagle, through the gates of Ghost Town.

Most of Lien's days, these last months, had been spent within the wall of Ghost Town, among the old Vinlanders, the "white ghosts." This was a bachelor society, with only one woman for every ten men. She'd gotten to know more than a few of them, over the long months, as nearly all of them had been involved in the construction of Gold Mountain, the three thousand kilometer-tall tower which rose to meet the orbital elevator, the Bridge of Heaven. Some of the old men had been more helpful than others. Some of them had reached such an advanced age that they couldn't even remember the year in which they were born, nor their own mothers' names. When asked, they would simply mutter, "It was too long, too long ago," in their guttural English. They were hollow men, these old Vinlanders, leaning against cold walls or sitting on empty fruit crates, patiently waiting for death to claim them. They were used up, discarded, and they made Lien uncomfortable in her own skin.

Lien had worked her whole life to overcome the stereotypes and misconceptions most Chinese had about Vinlanders, even those like her who had never set eyes on the homeland of their forefathers. Lien's grandfathers and one grandmother all arrived in China in the middle of the last century, and her father had been born in China. Ghost Town, full of men and women who fit every preconceived notion of the "white ghost," was a reminder to her of how far her people had come in China, and how far they had yet to go.

Lien had only been sent to Guangdong province because she spoke English, the native dialect of the Vinlanders. Her parents had insisted she learn the language, as her maternal grandparents had never learned Mandarin, nor Cantonese, nor any other Chinese dialect. She resented her grandparents for this, embarrassed by their refusal to acclimate. She seldom spoke to them when she and her sister were children, and even less as an adult. When her grandfather passed away, just the previous summer, she had not talked to him in nearly ten years. Lien didn't even attend the funeral ceremony, claiming that her duties at the Historical Bureau prevented her attendance. Her mother had yet to forgive her for this breech of etiquette.

Her last discussion with McAllister James had been brief, but he seemed more lucid and communicative than most of the old-timers she'd interviewed over the previous months. She anticipated a short discussion with him this morning, and with any luck she'd be back in Beijing by the week's end.

At the northern end of Ghost Town, Lien came to the building where her subject lived. To reach his small room on the top floor, Lien had to climb the rickety stairway, up passed the foul smelling Vinlander restaurant on the ground floor, from which the odor of grits, hominy and meatloaves constantly poured, and a small clinic on the second floor where a medicine man still tended to the injuries and ills of Ghost Town with his strange western remedies. At the top floor landing, she found herself at the end of a long, dimly lit hallway, with doorways crowded on either side. Lien checked her notes one final time, confirming the address, and made her way to the correct door.

The old man who answered the door looked at her with barely disguised suspicion, as though he didn't recognize her.

"Mister McAllister?" Lien said, speaking in English for the old man's benefit. "McAllister James? I am Johnston Lien, if you recall. We spoke last week at the market, and you agreed to speak with me for a brief while?"

The old man narrowed his watery eyes, and nodded slowly. Opening the door wide, he stepped out of the way, and motioned Lien inside. When she was through the door, he shut and locked it behind her, and then returned to a threadbare sofa in the far corner of the room. Lien crossed the dusty floorboards to a dining table and chair, the only other furniture in the room.

"May I be seated?"

The old man nodded, and Lien arranged herself on the chair, spreading her notes on the table in front of her.

"Thank you for agreeing to meet with me," Lien said, bowing slightly from the waist. The old man just watched her, his expression wary.

McAllister James, in his early eighties, matched the name of "ghost." He seemed spectral, intangible. The few hairs that remained on his liver-spotted scalp were wispy and white, his ears and nostrils grown enormous with the advancing years. He had only a few yellowed teeth left, stained by years of whisky and tobacco—the white man's vices. The skin of his face, neck, and arms was covered with the scars of the flowering-out disease, smallpox.

"You're going to pay, yes?" the old man said brusquely, the first words he'd spoken since she arrived. "To hear me talk?"

Lien nodded.

"Yes, there is a small honorarium, a few copper coins as fee for your trouble."

"Show me," he said.

With a sigh, Lien reached into her satchel, and withdrew a half dozen coppers, stamped with ideograms indicating good fortune, with a square hole bore through the middle. She arranged them in a neat tower at the corner of the table.

"There," Lien said. "Is that sufficient?"

The old man sat up slightly, peering over the edge of the table at the coins. He caught his lower lip between his gums, thinking it over for a moment.

"Alright," he grunted. "I'll talk."

"Very well, Mister McAllister. When we spoke at the market, last week, you mentioned that you were one of the first Vinlanders to come to China, and that you worked on Gold Mountain straight through to its completion. Is that correct?"

The old man leaned back, and arranged his skeletal hands in his lap.

"Well, I don't know that we were the first, but we must have been pretty damned near."

"We?"

The old man got a far away look in his eyes. A shadow passed briefly across his face, and then was gone.

"My brother and me," he explained. "We came here together, when we were young. And now there's just me, and I'm long past young."

My father was a sharecropper on a Tennessee cotton plantation, McAllister said, in Shelby County, just north and east of Memphis. The year the Chinaman came to town, we'd lost more than half of the crop to boll weevils, and we stood ready to starve. The Chinaman told us about work on the Gold Mountain, across the seas. Steady work and high pay for anyone who had a strong back and was willing. You didn't have to ask us twice. Michael—my brother—and I signed up on the spot, got a few pieces of copper for traveling expenses, and we were on our way.

Now, it wasn't that Michael and I were all hot on the notion of China. We liked things just fine in Tennessee, if there was money or work to be had. But there wasn't. In China, at least, we'd be fed three squares a day, and would make enough coin to send home to feed the rest of the family. Michael and I left our parents and two sisters behind, and went with the Chinaman down to the river, along with a dozen or so other young men from Shelby County. I never heard from my parents again, but a few years back my youngest sister's son wrote to me in Nine Dragons, inviting me to come back to Tennessee to live with them. By that time, though, Vinland was leaning a bit too close to the Aztec Empire for my taste, not under their rule but near enough as made no difference, and I didn't have any interest in living under the bloody shadow of the Mexica. No, I stayed right here in Ghost Town, where the only shadow that falls on me is that goddamned tower—Gold Mountain—and that line going up to heaven. We helped build that tower, my brother and me. It cost Michael his life, and cost me damn near everything else.

I was just eighteen when we rode that paddle steamer down the Mississippi to the Gulf of Mexica, where a China-bound freighter was waiting for us. Michael wasn't yet sixteen, and celebrated a birthday somewhere on the long sea voyage from the eastern shores of Vinland to the dock in Fragrant Harbor.

A lot of men died on the way over, though its not something a lot of us like to talk about. We were packed in the holds below deck cheek-to-jowl, and were lucky to get slop and water once a day. More often than not, though, the water had gone bad, or there were bugs in the slop, and what with the waves and the motion of the boat the food would either come back up or else rush too fast out the other end. When we rounded the tip of Fusang, down there in those cold reaches of the southern sea, the boat got to rocking so badly that our hold was near ankle deep in the spew and offal from the men. One man whose name I never knew shat himself to death, after swallowing amoebas or some such in the tainted water, but the ship's crew left his soiled corpse in the hold with us for nearly a week. When, years later, we finished construction on Gold Mountain, and work was scarce, a lot of men talked about going back to Vinland in one of those ships, taking their savings with them. I couldn't credit it, why anyone who'd been through an ocean voyage like that would willingly make another. I suppose that's one reason I stayed here in China, even after all that happened. I don't think the smell of those weeks has ever left my nostrils, not even these long decades later.

In any event, Michael and I made it to Guangdong more or less intact, where work was already underway on Gold Mountain. It was 1962 by our calendar, the 54th year of the Xuantong Emperor by the reckoning of the Chinese, and though Vinland had been a satellite state of China for just over a century, there'd been only a handful of Vinlanders who'd emigrated to China in all that time. I know Michael and I weren't the first to come, but we weren't too far behind.

Construction on Gold Mountain had begun the year before, from what I later learned. It hadn't taken long for the foreman and shift bosses to realize there weren't nearly enough willing laborers in China to meet the demands of the Ministry of Celestial Excursion. Hell, if they'd not sent out the call for workers to the ends of the Empire, they might still be building the tower even today. Some of those who came to work on Gold Mountain were from Africa, some from India, even a small number from Europe, but the most who answered the call were Vinlanders like Michael and me, mostly from the southern states of Tejas, Tennessee, Kentuck and Oklahoma.

Gold Mountain wasn't much taller than a regular building, at that point. Up on the hill called Great Peace—on the western end of the island of Fragrant Harbor, just across the bay from the Nine Dragons Peninsula—it was a boxy framework of graphite epoxy about a kilometer on a side, and just a few hundred meters tall. They'd not even pressurized the bottom segments yet, just laid the foundation. By the time we were through, that tower reached up three thousand kilometers, and all because of us. Chinese minds might have dreamed the thing, but it was the sweat off Vinlander backs that built it. That, and Vinlander blood.

But even then, at the beginning, we knew we weren't really welcome. The Chinese called Vinlanders "white ghosts," and said we were barbarians, and savages, and worse. And even when we moved from Guangdong into the other provinces, after Gold Mountain was built, we'd still be huddled together into Ghost Towns at the fringes of town, welcome only to run restaurants, or do bureaucrats' laundry, or manual labor.

When we got off the freighter at the Fragrant Harbor dock, it was just chaos. Two other ships were letting out workers, and there must have been hundreds, thousands even, all packed into that small space. None of us knew where to go, or what to do, most of us too busy trying to remember how to walk on dry land to be of much use to anyone. There were men in loose fitting white jackets and pants, standing on upturned boxes, calling out in a dozen different languages. One of them was a white man speaking English with a Tejas accent. He said, "All Vinlanders who want to work, come with me!" I grabbed Michael by the arm, and we followed the man into the city.

Fragrant Harbor wasn't then like it is today. What Chinese there were in the area all lived across the bay in Nine Dragons, and all of the government offices, and restaurants and shops and such were over there with them. In Fragrant Harbor there wasn't much besides the docks, the warehouses where all the building materials were kept, and the Gold Mountain worksite. All of the workers were housed in a tent city on the east side of Great Peace mountain. Like tended to attract like, so one part of the tent city would be Swedes, another part Ethiops, another part Hindi. When Michael and I arrived, there weren't but a few hundred Vinlanders in the whole place, all huddled together in one corner of the tent city. By the time Gold Mountain was complete, and they shut down the worksite, we numbered in the thousands, and tens of thousands.

The work was hard, and dangerous, even before the tower climbed kilometers into the sky. The lattice of Gold Mountain is made up of pressurized segments filled with pressurized gas. That's what gives the tower its strength, what lets it stand so tall. Without those segments to distribute tension and weight, we couldn't have built a tower much taller than 400 kilometers, much less high enough to hook up with the orbital tether of the Bridge of Heaven. But the same thing that made the tower possible made it damnably tricky to build. God help you if you were up on a scaffolding or on a rig when a bulkhead blew out, or if you were down below when the graphite epoxy debris of an explosive depressurization rained down like shrapnel. And then, once the tower was tall enough, you didn't have to worry just about a bulkhead exploding in your face, or you loosing your grip and falling down a thousand meters below, but you had to start worrying about your supply of heated oxygen running out, or your pressure suit catching a leak, or your thermals failing and your fingers and toes freezing before you could get to safety. There weren't many in Ghost Town once Gold Mountain was through that hadn't lost at least a finger or toe to the chill of two thousand kilometers up, and there weren't any that hadn't buried what was left of a friend—or a brother—who'd fallen off the tower to their untimely end. I've buried my share, and then some.

It wasn't all work, though, even when things were at their hardest. There was a good living, in those early days, to be made off of the appetites of the Vinlander workers. Most of us didn't trust eastern medicine, and wouldn't put our health in the hands of an herbalist if our lives depended on it, so the foremen of the worksite would hire sawbones, Vinlanders and Europeans with experience in Western medicine to see to our health and well-being. And when we got hungry, we wanted food that reminded us of home, not the fish-heads and strange fruits of the Chinaman. The first restaurateurs were Vinlanders who realized they could make a better living feeding their fellow workers traditional southern fare—grits, hominy, meatloaves and cornbread—than they could working at construction themselves.

Less savory aspects of the Vinlanders' appetites, too, were met by the brothels. Owned by Chinese businessmen, these would bring young girls from Vinland to "service" the workers. Most were damned near slaves, sold into indentured servitude by their parents back in Vinland for a few coins. Their contracts ran for ten years, at the end of which they would be free. Rare was the woman who made it ten years in the brothels.

Michael—god rest his soul—lost his heart to one of those girls in the Excelsior Saloon and Brothel. She was from Tejas, and her name was Susanne Greene, or Greene Zhu Xan as the Chinawoman madame called her. Michael fell in love with her on sight. For my sins, I suppose I fell in love with her, too. We'd been in China just two years, and the tower now reached several kilometers into the sky. Since our arrival, we'd been sending back home at least one in every ten coins we made. Once Michael met Zhu Xan, though, he had other uses for his money. Not prurient uses, mind, though he was a frequent enough visitor to the Excelsior. No, he was saving up his money to buy Zhu Xan out of her contract at the brothel, so he could take her for his wife.

Well, Michael had just about gotten his nut together when we made that last ascent. We were line-and-basket men, Michael and me, always working high up in the scaffolds, welding together the joints in the latticework and securing the bulkheads. We were at the very top, must have been seven or eight kilometers up, and we had to wear heavy thermal suits and breathing apparatuses just to be up there. Michael was in the basket that day, while I was up on the joist working the rigging.

I can't rightly say what went wrong. One minute I was up there looking out over the pale blue sky as it stretched out over the curve of the horizon, and the next minute I heard a sound like a musket shot, and all hell broke loose. By the time I looked down, as quick as it takes to say it, everything had changed. The line had separated just above the basket, just snapped in two like a string pulled too tight, and there was Michael, hanging onto the side of the scaffold for dear life. The basket was tumbling down to the ground far below. It fell straight for a ways, spinning slightly end over end, but then it bumped against the side of the tower and was sent spiraling out, away from the scaffold. I lost sight of it in a cloud bank. The top of the line, the end still attached to the rigging, snapped back towards me like a whip, and almost caught me across the chest. As it was, I managed to shy away just in time, but it slapped against the joist as loud as a thunderclap, and left a mark in that graphite epoxy, which isn't an easy material to scuff.

Now, the gloves and boots on those thermal suits weren't made for climbing, but Michael did his level best. The walls of the tower were just an empty framework of girders that high up, without bulkhead walls, and so he was able to worm his slow way back up to the top. He wasn't much more than a few dozen meters below the top when the basket-line broke, and he managed to climb a few meters before his strength gave out. Then he was left hanging there, his arms wrapped around a girder, calling through his helmet radio for help.

He was calling for me, calling for his brother, begging me to come down and help him. And I could have, too. I could have attached a safety line to my suit's harness, and repelled down and taken his hand. It wouldn't have taken more than a few minutes. I could have lowered myself, grabbed hold of Michael, and then raised us both back up to safety. But I didn't.

I want to say that I couldn't, but that's not true. I could have done, if I'd not been a coward. I'd never known that I was a coward before that moment, but seeing my brother dangling over the abyss, and knowing that the only thing standing between him and the Almighty was me, I just froze with fear, unable to move. I just stayed where I was, holding onto the joist for all I was worth, trying to shut out the sounds of Michael's calls for help in my helmet's speakers.

When Michael fell, I heard his screams, all the way down.

When I got back down to Earth, the first thing I did was hie myself over to the Excelsior, to break the news to Zhu Xan. With Michael gone, I figured I'd do the right thing and offer to marry her, myself. As his next of kin, Michael's savings would be mine, and I could think of no fitter use for that sad legacy than to buy the freedom of the woman he'd loved.

By the time I walked through the swinging doors of the Excelsior, though, it was already too late. Michael fell far faster than I could climb down, and gossip flies even faster still, so word of her lover's fall had reached Zhu Xan's ears long before I arrived. There, in the big front parlor of the Excelsior, I saw the broken and lifeless body of Zhu Xan, past all caring. She'd jumped from the balcony of one of the upper rooms, and fallen to her death in the street far below, a tintype of Michael McAllister clutched to her breast. The whores and drunkards of the saloon had brought her body inside, where it lay in state, like she was some departed queen. They were buried in the workers' cemetery that night, Zhu Xan and what little remained of Michael, side by side in a narrow trench.

I never again ascended the heights of Gold Mountain. I begged the foremen to let me work on the ground. My terror and cowardice had already cost my brother his life, and I didn't want to put myself, or anyone else, at risk ever again. I spent the next twelve years on the ground, hauling slag, moving girders and bulkhead walls and gas canisters, while above me the tower of Gold Mountain rose ever higher, its shadow growing longer and longer with every passing day.

I was thirty-seven years old when Gold Mountain was complete, and the Bridge of Heaven tether reached down from the orbital platform to the top of the three thousand kilometer tower. Heaven and earth were joined together, and man could ride the Bridge of Heaven thirty six thousand kilometers to orbit.

With work on Gold Mountain complete, the Vinlanders were left without jobs. Some of us returned to Vinland, taking what little they'd been able to save with them—a pittance in China, but a fortune back in Mule Shoe, or Memphis, or Augusta—but most lost even that little in the gambling dens, or over cards or dice on the long sea voyage home. Provided they made it back alive, that is, since many died in the passage, with money still in their pockets, through sickness, or injury, or misadventure.

Some Vinlanders found work in factories, or in mills, or on fishing trawlers, wherever there was hard work to be done that the Chinese didn't want to do. They moved from the coastal region of Guangdong to the other provinces of China, living in small enclaves of "white ghosts," eking out hardscrabble livings.

I stayed in Guangdong, for my part. With the worksite closed, we that remained settled across the bay in Nine Dragons, and took what work we could find. There was a wall in Ghost Town where Vinlanders posted messages and notices, and we'd haunt that corner, looking for word of jobs, of any work. But there weren't just work notices. There'd be desperate notes from fathers searching for their sons, or brothers for brothers. Or else warnings not to take work with a particular farmer or mill owner, those that did not pay promised wages or who provided their workers food unfit for consumption. Old men, towermen from the earliest days of Gold Mountain—most of them short a few fingers and toes, some of them missing arms and legs—would sit on upturned fruit crates in the street, and read the posted notices to those who couldn't read for themselves.

The gangs and mutual protection societies flourished in those days, usually made up of men from the same state or region of Vinland. The Lone Stars of Tejas, the Okies of Oklahoma, the Cardinals of Kentucky. I never had much patience for that sort of thing, myself, but knew enough not to cross any of them. If a Lone Star wanted your seat at the bar, you best give it to him, if you wanted the use of all your limbs by the next day. But they lived by their own sort of code, and if you did right by them, they'd do right by you.

There were gambling dens in Ghost Town, too, as there'd been in the Gold Mountain tent city. Places were men shot dice or played cards, bet on the outcome of dog fights and cock fights, boxing matches and tests of skill. Many lost a month's salary in a single night's indiscretion, though I suppose there must have been a few to see a profit out of it.

Many, too, spent their wages in the whisky dens, where Chinamen and women of position and standing could sometimes be found, lounging on hardwood benches, smoking thick-rolled cigars and sipping Tennessee whisky or Kentuck bourbon. The Chinese came to soak up the local color, and get an amusing story about their night among the savages to tell the folks back home.

I still had a healthy bankroll, what with my own savings, and those left me after Michael's death. I rented a suite of rooms in the nicer quarter of Ghost Town, and got a good paying job as a shift manager at a cigar-rolling factory. All of the factory workers were Southern Vinlanders, and the owner of the factory was a Mandarin who was kind to his workers, when his mood was right. When his mood was dark, he could be as fierce as a demon from hell, but thankfully those times were few and far between.

Things were good, for a few years, but it all changed when I got the smallpox, the "flowering-out disease." I lost my job, and damn near lost my life. Most of us who caught the disease died of it, and those that survived will bear the scars of it for the rest of our days. We didn't trust Chinese herbalists, of course, so we trusted our fates to the hands of Vinlander sawbones, practitioners who had little experience with the disease, and were ill-equipped to treat it. By the time I was past the worst of it, weak and scarred, I'd spent nearly all of my savings on medicines. I'd been shut out of the cigar factory, to keep from spreading the disease to the others, and when my savings ran dry I was evicted from my suite and turned out on the street. I was 42 years old, and had to start all over, from the bottom.

I found work in a garment shop, stitching the hems on women's robes. My wages were enough that I could rent a small room, and eat regularly, but not much more besides. I'd not sent home any money in years, by this point, and was still plagued with the guilt of it from time to time. I sometimes wondered what had become of my parents. Surely they were dead by now. Had they known somehow what had become of Michael, or died thinking that he still lived, somewhere across the sea?

Things weren't going much better for the rest of the Vinlanders in China, either. In the popular press, we were described as heathens and barbarians. They said we were savage, impure, full of strange lusts and foreign diseases. There were new decrees issued every year—no Chinese could marry a white, no white could own property, no white could take imperial examination—just to keep us in line.

Things reached a head ten years after the completion of Gold Mountain. The Council of Deliberative Officials enacted an Exclusion Decree that said no more Vinlanders could enter China. The wives and families of current resident laborers like me were barred from entry. All Vinlanders needed to be registered, and to carry our papers at all times. Only Vinlanders who were teachers, merchants, students, or diplomats would be permitted entry, and there were scarce few of those.

Then came the Driving Out, as the Vinlanders who had moved to the other regions of China were forced out, at the point of a sword or the barrel of a musket. There had been Ghost Towns in most large Chinese cities in the years after the Bridge of Heaven was completed, but after the Exclusion Decree, the only one left was in Nine Dragons.

Some Vinlanders formed partnerships of up to ten men, pooling their money to open businesses that would let them claim status as "merchants." They could then receive a certificate of legal residency, instead of being considered itinerant laborers. I tried to pool my money with a pair of brothers named Jefferson and their cousins, to open a dry goods store in Ghost Town, but in the end the ties of family proved stronger than any other obligation. The brothers, with the help of one of their cousins, falsified documents to cut me out of the partnership, swindling me of all my savings, and leaving me worse off than I'd been before. I was nearing fifty, and fit only for manual labor.

It has been more than thirty years since, nearly half of a Chinese cycle of years, and I'm still in virtually the same position as I was then. Since coming to work on Gold Mountain, I made two small fortunes, at least as far as Vinlanders are concerned, and lost them both. I've never since made near that much. Perhaps my heart hasn't been in it. Or two chances were all I had, in this lifetime, and having used them both my only choice is to wait until the next world, or the next life, whichever the case may be. My only regret, I suppose, is that I never married, but with so few Vinlander women in the country, I didn't have much choice. Too bad that Zhu Xan couldn't have waited, just a few minutes more, to take that leap from the Excelsior's balcony. Perhaps we could have been happy together. I think about her still, from time to time. And my brother, of course.

The Exclusion Decree was repealed, fifteen years after it was enacted, but the fact that Vinlanders can now immigrate to China with more ease means little to us old bachelors of Ghost Town. I will die without ever laying eyes on my homeland again. The world has passed us by. We wait. We will welcome Death when he comes.

In the vestibule, commuters bustled, waiting for the bell that would sound the arrival of the next gondola. Just beyond the doors, the electromagnetic rails ran straight up the side of the tower, climbing up past the clouds. To one side of the room stood a young woman of Vinlander extraction, and a very old white ghost.

Johnston Lien and McAllister James were on the island of Fragrant Harbor, standing in the departure lounge at the base station of Gold Mountain. The old man was nervous, his gaze darting about the room furtively, his arms tucked in close to his narrow chest. Lien had not told him why they'd come, only that she had a surprise for him. In the end, she had to promise McAllister another stack of copper coins before he'd leave his rented rooms, and only with them safely in hand would he agree to bestir himself.

Lien had stayed in Guangdong longer than she'd expected. She could have left the week before, after finishing her interview with McAllister, but after hearing his story, she felt there was one more thing she had to do.

She was reminded of her grandfather, to look at McAllister now. Her own grandfather might have been such a man, had he not married her grandmother, and raised a family, and opened a successful Vinlander restaurant in Guangdong during the years of the Exclusion Decree, and later moved north to serve his cuisine in the capital city, and once even served a distant cousin of the emperor himself, and died in bed surrounded by friends and family. Except for an ungrateful granddaughter, of course, who never considered what sacrifices her parents and grandparents might have made so that she could grow up in a China where she could take imperial examinations, and hold administrative office. Women couldn't yet own property, or remarry after the death of their husbands, but Lien was sure that was just a matter of time.

By the same token, had circumstances been other than they were, McAllister might have been her grandfather. He was of the right age, and background, and had it been he that met her grandmother, then things might have gone quite differently for him.

She had allowed her grandfather to slip from this life without taking the opportunity to say a final farewell, nor to thank him. Perhaps in doing some small favor for McAllister James, she could make amends to her grandfather's spirit. She'd had to pull strings at the Ministry of Celestial Excursion, and there was a regional administrator whom she now owed a significant favor, but Lien was convinced it was worth it. For McAllister's sake, for that of her grandfather, and for Lien herself. She felt calmer and more at peace at this moment than she had in years, anxious to see the look on the old man's face.

"Why we here?" the old man finally asked, in his broken Cantonese.

"You'll see," Lien answered in English, laying a gentle hand on the old man's shoulder.

The departure bell chimed as the gondola approached, and the doors opened with a hissing outrush of air once the gondola was safely docked.

"Come along, Mister McAllister." Lien took his withered hand in hers, and gently lead him toward the open doors.

The old man's eyes darted from side to side, as he meekly followed behind.

"Where are we going?" he asked in English.

"You'll see."

The gondola doors slid closed behind them, and Lien guided the old man to an open acceleration couch. There were a few dozen engineers, naval officers and bureaucrats in the gondola with them, and a number of them cast sidelong glances at the old white man trembling in the corner, some with thinly disguised contempt.

The acceleration couch offered an unobstructed view of the observation ports on the opposite wall of the gondola. The old man looked to the window, confused, and it was not until the ground fell away, and he saw the rooftops of Fragrant Harbor spread out like a embroidered quilt at his feet, that he understood what was happened.

"No," he said, his voice soft and far away. "Too high. Too long ago. No."

Lien took his hand in hers, and tried to sooth him.

"It will be alright, Mister McAllister. The Bridge of Heaven is perfectly safe."

The view out the gondola window was now of the bay, and of the Nine Dragons Peninsula. To the north stretched Guangdong and the Chinese mainland, to the east and south the sapphire blue of the south China sea.

"Oh, no," the old man said, squeezing his eyes shut tight. "Too long."

In moments, the gondola was ascending at speeds of one thousand kilometers per hour, then two thousand kph, then faster still. On either side of the passenger gondola, cargo loads traveling up and down the tether at speeds of over thirty-nine thousand kph rocketed by, exerting hundreds of thousands of gees on the cargoes they carried, enough to liquefy any passengers. At its leisurely top speed of three thousand kph, still putting several gees of pressure on its occupants, it would take the passenger gondola just over twelve hours to reach Diamond Summit, the station in geosynchronous Earth orbit above Fragrant Harbor.

"No," the old man said, shaking his head.

Lien was beside herself.

"I'm *so* sorry!" she said, squeezing McAllister's frail hand as hard as she dared. "I'd thought to do something nice for you. I'd no idea you'd be so frightened."

"No," the old man whispered urgently.

"It will be alright," Lien insisted. "Once we get to the top, you'll see what I wanted to show you, and then we can return. Alright? Please forgive me, I didn't mean to cause you distress."

The old man kept silent, his mouth drawn into a line, and turned his head away.

By the third hour, the old man would not speak to Lien, not even in response to direct questions. He just sat, his hands in white-knuckled grips on the straps of the couch, his gaze fixed on the curve of the horizon visible through the viewport. When the stewards came by to serve the mid-voyage meal, the old man waved them away, accepting only a bulb of water from their trays.

When the gondola slowed, and docked at Diamond Summit, the passengers found themselves weightless. The stewards helped them from their couches, and guided them to the nose of the gondola, to the airlock that led to the Diamond Summit entryway.

Once onboard Diamond Summit, Lien led the old man to the main body of the station, which rotated around the central hub, providing artificial gravity to the environs. At a large reinforced panoramic window the pair stopped.

In front of them, a few thousand kilometers off, they could see the last of the Treasure Fleet departing for the red planet Fire Star. Below them stretched the blue curve of the Earth, and the glow of the sun limning the far horizon with pale fire. They could see even as far as the edge of the western hemisphere, and the northern continent which McAllister had once called home. Nearest them was the Muslim colony of Khalifa on the coast, founded in centuries past by admirals of the Dragon Throne. Beyond that, off towards the blazing sun in the east, rose the lands of the Commonwealth of Vinland.

"There," Lien said, supporting the old man with one arm, pointing towards the distant horizon with the other. "That is what I wanted to show you. First to let you see what your labor those many long years was for, and second to give you a final look at your lost home. There, on the horizon. That is your . . . that is *our* homeland. Vinland."

The old man was trembling. He looked from the panorama to Lien, his eyes watering and his lip quivering.

"You . . . you don't understand," he managed to get out, with difficulty. His voice caught in his throat, sounding like an injured bullfrog. "It's not terror that plagues me, but guilt."

Lien looked at the old man, confused.

"But I assumed that you were still afflicted by the fear that gripped you up on Gold Mountain, all those years ago."

The old man jerked his head from side to side, as though trying to shake her words from his ears.

"No!" he shouted, flecks of foam spotting the corners of his mouth. "It wasn't fear, not even then. You don't . . . "

He left off for a moment, pulling away from Lien and averting his eyes.

Lien reached out and laid a hand on his thin shoulder. She thought of her grandfather, and all that had gone unsaid between them.

"Please," she said. "Tell me."

"No," he repeated, with less conviction.

"Please," she urged. "What do you mean it wasn't fear?"

The old man turned to her, his face a red grimace, his eyes flashing.

"It was envy!" he said. "It was lust! It was greed! But it was never fear. Anything but fear!"

He rocked back on his heels, eyes on the far ceiling, his body racked with sobs.

"I could have saved Michael," he went on. "I only had to reach out my hand. But as he dangled there, I couldn't help thinking that with him gone, Zhu Xan would be mine. I loved her, just as he did, and with my brother dead the way would be clear for me. But . . . "

He broke off again, sobs interrupting his words. He slid to the floor, on his knees, his hands in his lap.

"But she was already dead," Lien said.

Mucus ran down his face, and tears streamed across his dry cheeks. "Yes!" he wailed.

Lien stood, looking down at the frail old man at her feet, rocked by paroxysm of grief and guilt.

"That's why you never went home, isn't it?" she asked, realization dawning. "Why you never returned to Vinland. You couldn't face your family."

The old man nodded, and beat his thin fists against the carpeted floor. "Yes!" he shouted.

Without another word, she knelt down, and wrapped her arms around the old man's slender frame. She drew him tight to her, and McAllister pressed his face into her shoulder, convulsing with sobs.

"Oh, Michael!" the old man said, his voice cracking. "I'm so, so sorry. It was my job to protect you, and I . . . Oh, God. Forgive me. Forgive me!"

Lien held him tighter, and stroked the back of his wrinkled skull with her hand.

"I forgive you," she whispered, tears in her eyes.

They held each other, the old white ghost and the woman from the Northern Capital. Diamond Summit turned, and the curve of Vinland slipped out of view, and the mountains and plains of China swelled to fill the window.

"Now, grandfather," Lien said, at the edge of hearing. "Forgive me, too."

First published in *Postscripts,* Autumn 2005

ABOUT THE AUTHOR _____

Chris Roberson is probably best known for his Alternate History "Celestrial Empire" series, which, in addition to a large number of short pieces (including "Gold Mountain"), consists of the novels *The Dragon's Nine Sons, Iron Jaw and Hummingbird, The Voyage of Night Shining White,* and *Three Unbroken.* His other novels include, *Here, There & Everywhere, Paragaea: A Planetary Romance, Set the Seas on Fire, Voices of Thunder, Cybermany, Incorporated, Any Time At All, End of the Century, Book of Secrets,* and *Further: Beyond the*

Threshhold, and he has also contributed to the "Warhammer," "X-Men," and "Shark Boy and Lava Girl" series, and written "Elric" graphic novels in collaboration with Michael Moorcock. In addition to his writing, Robertson is one of the publishers of the lively small press MonkeyBrain Books, and edited the "retro-pulp" anthology *Adventure, Volume 1.* He won the Sidewise Award for Best Alternate History in 2004 with his story "O One." Roberson lives with his family in Austin, Texas.

The Issue of Gender in Genre Fiction: Publications from Slush

SUSAN E. CONNOLLY

The issue of representation of men and women in science fiction is one that has caused much discussion. There's "The Count," from Strange Horizons which looks at professional reviews of science fiction novels by gender, and a similar initiative by Lady Business for blog reviews. A common query when it comes to this issue of representation is the makeup of submissions. Are the differences we see simply reflections of the proportion of submissions received?

There has been some investigation of this question before, and by widening the data-gathering net, I hope to allow a more nuanced and informed discussion of the issue. I have also attempted to perform separate analyses of submissions as a whole, as well as science fiction submissions specifically.

In the previous article I looked at the gender ratios of published stories of all genres and published science fiction stories in seventeen SFWA short fiction markets. While looking at published fiction alone does give us some important information about the gender representation of authors both overall and between different markets, it's not the end of things. In addition to gathering data on published stories, I asked editors for details of the source of those published stories.

With some editors receiving hundreds of submissions every week, the effort and time to categorize even a sample of those submissions for this study was substantial, and I am extremely grateful for that assistance.

Publications from Slush

Some markets draw all of their published stories from open submissions, while others draw from a combination of slush submissions, reprints, and stories solicited from authors. For the second group, it is useful to compare the published stories with those that came from slush, to see if this results in significantly different gender ratios. After all, it could be the case that reprints or solicited stories show a different kind of gender ratio than the stories that just come from slush.

Those markets which drew published stories from outside the slush pile during the period studied were: *Apex, Clarkesworld, Daily Science Fiction, Escape Pod, F&SF, F&SF* Special Issue, *Lightspeed, Strange Horizons,* and *Tor.com.*

Table 1: Reprints and Solicited Stories Status of Markets

Market	Solicit Stories	Publish Reprints	Notes
AE	Yes	No	All stories came from slush in 2013.
Analog	No	No	
Apex	Yes	Yes	On investigation, the numbers for Apex in the previous article were slightly off. (17 Men, 28 Women, 1 Non-Binary, 1 Unknown.) This has been corrected for this piece to 18 Men, 27 Women, and 2 Non-Binary.) Apex editors also did not assign genres to speculative fiction, so the division was based on my own assessment. Reprints data for SF stories was available, but data for solicited stories was not.
Asimov's	No	No	
Bull Spec	Yes	Yes	All stories came from slush in 2013.
Buzzy Mag	No	No	
Clarkesworld	No	Yes	

Daily Science Fiction	Yes	No	
Escape Pod	Yes	Yes	
F&SF	Yes	Yes	
F&SF Special Issue	Yes	No	
Flash Fiction Online	No	No	
IGMS	No	No	
Lightspeed	No	Yes	
Nature	No	No	
Strange Horizons	No	Yes	
Tor.com	Yes	No	

Taking this subset of markets and graphing Publications from Slush vs Total Publications, we can see that reprints and solicited stories make up a large proportion of published fiction in some markets. When looking at the percentage share of each gender, there are some slight differences when comparing Publications from Slush with Total Publications for both all stories and science fiction stories.

However, *overall*, the differences in ratios between **All Published Stories** and **Stories from Slush** *are not significant.*

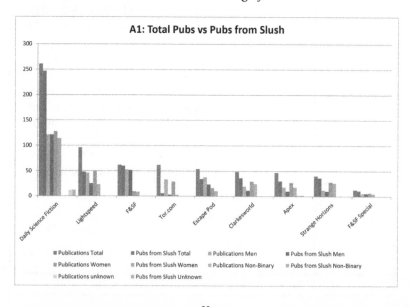

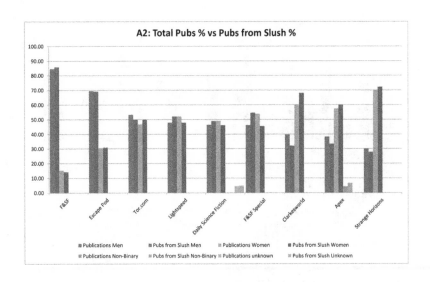

A2: Total Pubs % vs Pubs from Slush %

Legend: Publications Men · Pubs from Slush Men · Publications Women · Pubs from Slush Women · Publications Non-Binary · Pubs from Slush Non-Binary · Publications unknown · Pubs from Slush Unknown

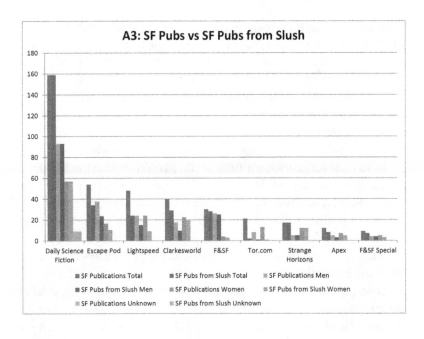

A3: SF Pubs vs SF Pubs from Slush

Legend: SF Publications Total · SF Pubs from Slush Total · SF Publications Men · SF Pubs from Slush Men · SF Publications Women · SF Pubs from Slush Women · SF Publications Unknown · SF Pubs from Slush Unknown

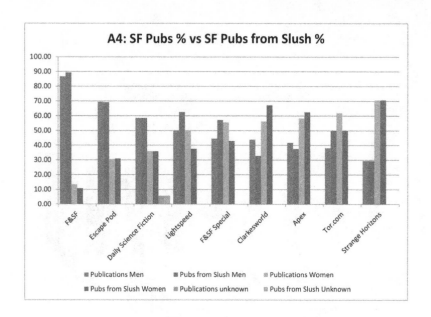

A4: SF Pubs % vs SF Pubs from Slush %

Legend:
- Publications Men
- Pubs from Slush Men
- Publications Women
- Pubs from Slush Women
- Publications unknown
- Pubs from Slush Unknown

Submissions: Samples and Variation

As mentioned in the previous article, please note that this is a study of apparent gender. Some editors used Google to obtain public bios of the authors for a more accurate categorization of author gender, and some were already aware of the gender identity of some authors, but in most cases the categorization by gender was based on first name. This inherently makes the gender split less accurate than it was in the previous article.

Additionally, when dealing with overall publications and comparing them to publications drawn from slush, I could look at the full dataset for the time period. However, with some publications receiving thousands of submissions per year, many markets were understandably unable to provide full breakdowns for a year's worth of submissions. As such, I am dealing with samples from varying time periods. This means that the analysis will not be quite as comprehensive or accurate as would be ideal.

Drawing conclusions about the yearly submissions from a smaller sample may lead to error. For example, *Escape Pod* provided data for the months of February 2014, April 2014, and May 2014. We can see a variation of 4.01% between the highest and lowest months in terms of gender ratios.

Table 2: *Escape Pod* Submissions by Month

	Total Submissions	Submissions from Men	Submissions from Women
February	85	65	20
		76.47%	23.53%
April	69	50	19
		72.46%	27.54%
May	70	53	17
		75.71%	24.29%
Average	74.67	56	18.67
		75%	25%

Looking at a separate twelve month period of *Clarkesworld Magazine*'s submissions, we can see additional evidence of variation in gender ratios. This chart looks at both total submissions (including science fiction, fantasy, horror, science fiction/fantasy and science fiction/horror) and science fiction subs only (including science fiction, science fiction/fantasy and science fiction/horror.)

While the overall breakdown for the year was 71.06% men and 28.94% women for *all* submissions, the highest month for representation of men came in at 73.19%, and the lowest at 69.62%. This gives us a 3.57% difference between the months with the highest and lowest representation of men. So, we can see that a one-month sample would not have accurately reflected the yearly ratios.

Table 3: *Clarkesworld* Submissions Gender Ratio Variation

	Overall		High		Low		High-Low Diff.
	Men	Women	Men	Women	Men	Women	
Total Subs	71.06%	28.94%	73.19%	26.81%	69.62%	30.38%	3.57%
SF Subs	75.29%	24.71%	77.21%	22.79%	73.58%	26.42%	3.63%

We also see variation in overall volume of submissions, as detailed below. (In all cases but the highest volume of total subs by women, the highs/lows in volume by gender were also found in the same month as for overall submissions.) Again, we can see that while the average (mean) month had 776 submissions, with 551 by men and 224 by women, one month had 933 submissions total, while one had only 649.

Table 4: *Clarkesworld* Submissions Volume Variation

	Average			High			Low		
	Total	Men	Women	Total	Men	Women	Total	Men	Women
Total Subs Vol.	776	551	224	933	657	278	649	475	174
SF Subs Vol.	403	303	100	517	381	136	338	259	79

Given these variations, it is likely that the submission samples are not giving a completely accurate representation of the overall yearly ratios, so any kind of specific ranking of markets based on the ratios given here would not be a good idea. That said, we can likely still draw tentative generalized conclusions.

Overall, I have data for fourteen of the seventeen markets when it comes to submissions for all genres, and twelve of the seventeen markets for science fiction submissions.

Table 5: Submissions Data Provided By Markets

Market	All Stories Sample	SF Stories Sample	Notes
AE	150 submissions of the 503 total for 2013.	150 submissions of the 503 total for 2013	
Analog	Read and replied for thirty days during the months of Jan. and Feb. 2014	Read and replied for thirty days during the months of Jan. and Feb. 2014.	This market did not look at the submissions that were *received* in a certain time period, but rather at the submissions which were *replied* to.

Apex	Read and replied from Jan. 1st 2014 - Feb. 18th 2014. (Sample 1)	Read and replied from Jan. 1st 2014 - Feb. 18th 2014. (Sample 2)	This market did not look at the submissions that were *received* in a certain time period, but rather at the submissions which were *replied* to.
Asimov's	Read and replied for thirty days during the months of Dec. and Jan. 2014.	No submissions data available	This market did not look at the submissions that were *received* in a certain time period, but rather at the submissions which were *replied* to. The number of submissions closed in this time period was unusually high, but the gender ratios are in accordance with the yearly total for closed submissions.
Bull Spec	a) Total number of submissions for last open subs. b) Submissions received Oct. 1st - Oct. 10th and Nov. 1st - Nov. 5th.	Submissions received Oct. 1st - Oct.10th and Nov. 1st - Nov. 5th.	Last open Subs were the months of Oct. and Nov., 2011
Buzzy Mag	No submissions data available.	No submissions data available.	
Clarkesworld	Submissions received for year seven which ranged from Oct. 2012 - Oct. 2013.	Submissions received for year seven which ranged from Oct. 2012 - Oct. 2013.	*Clarkesworld* tracks submissions in the categories of SF, F, H, SF/F, and SF/Horror. SF, SF/F and SF/H were considered as SF for this study. (In general, editors divided submissions based on a broad definition of SF)

Daily Science Fiction	Three weeks of submissions during Feb. 2014.	No submissions data available.	
Escape Pod	Stories read in Feb., May, and Apr. 2014.	Stories read in Feb., May, and Apr. 2014.	This market did not look at the submissions that were *received* in a certain time period, but rather at the submissions which were *read*.
F&SF	No submissions data available.	No submissions data available.	
F&SF Special Issue	All submissions in open period from Jan. 1st - Jan. 14th.	All submissions in open period from Jan. 1st - Jan. 14th 2014.	
Flash Fiction Online	a) Total number of submissions in 2013. b) Submissions received Oct. 2013.	Submissions received Oct. 2013.	Oct. 2013 was an unusually busy month. Editor based count on author's submission tag, but estimates that another 7-10% of submissions could be considered science fiction.
IGMS	a) Total submissions for year 2013. b) Submissions received Jan. 2014 (Sample 2)	a) Submissions received Apr. 2013. (Sample 1) b) Submissions received Jan. 2014. (Sample 2)	

Lightspeed	Total submissions for 2013.	Total submissions for 2013.	Lightspeed was open to submissions in June and July of 2013. While closed to slush, there was a backdoor for authors Lightspeed had previously published/solicited. Submissions data from that portal was incorporated into these results. This doesn't include any data from the Women Destroy Science Fiction special issue, which opened to submissions Dec. 15, 2013.
Nature	Total submissions for 2013.	Total submissions for 2013.	
Strange Horizons	Two weeks of 2013, six months apart.	Two weeks of 2013, six months apart.	
Tor.com	No submissions data available	No submissions data available	

Submissions Volume

In addition to looking at the proportions of submissions by gender, it is also interesting to look at the number of submissions received by each market. There is a wide disparity between the volume of submissions received by each market. In order to give an indication of this, markets that gave only a sample of submissions were brought to a one year volume for comparison. This is only a rough comparison; in addition to the variability between different time periods mentioned earlier, some of these markets may be closed to submissions at various points.

The deficiencies of this method of estimation can be seen by comparing the actual total submissions with the estimate from the sample, in the markets where we have both values: *Flash Fiction Online*, *IGMS*, and *Bull Spec*. This has some impact on certain statistical tests (e.g. chi-square) but does not necessarily invalidate most of the results found here.

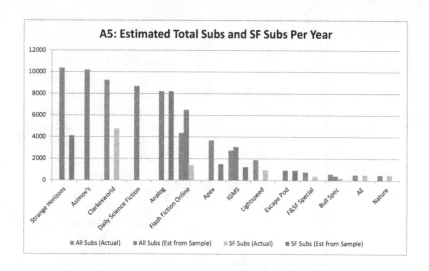

A5: Estimated Total Subs and SF Subs Per Year

■ All Subs (Actual)   ■ All Subs (Est from Sample)   ■ SF Subs (Actual)   ■ SF Subs (Est from Sample)

Submissions Ratios

Overall, we see a much smaller degree of variance between markets with Submissions than we saw with Publications.

All Submissions

Range: Submissions by Men: 81.31% to 54.59% = 26.72%
Range: Submissions by Women: 18.69% to 45.41% = 26.72%
The mean ratios are 67.94% men, 29.63% women, 0.02% non-binary and 2.43% unknown.
The median ratios are 68.40% men, 29.55% women, 0% non-binary and 0% unknown.

Science Fiction Submissions

Range: Submissions by Men: 81.31% to 58.67% = 22.64%
Range: Submissions by Women: 18.69% to 41.27% = 22.58%
The mean ratios are 70.92% men, 27.52% women, and 1.61% unknown.
The median ratios are 72.65% men, 25.89% women, and 0% unknown.

Note: For ease of comparison between All Subs and Science Fiction Subs (where possible), the source of the data is indicated in the label for each market.

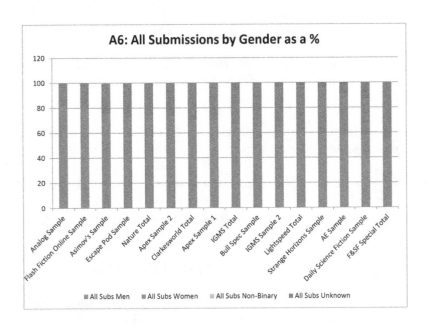

A6: All Submissions by Gender as a %

Analog Sample, Flash Fiction Online Sample, Asimov's Sample, Escape Pod Sample, Nature Total, Apex Sample 2, Clarkesworld Total, Apex Sample 1, IGMS Total, Bull Spec Sample, IGMS Sample 2, Lightspeed Total, Strange Horizons Sample, AE Sample, Daily Science Fiction Sample, F&SF Special Total

■ All Subs Men   ■ All Subs Women   ■ All Subs Non-Binary   ■ All Subs Unknown

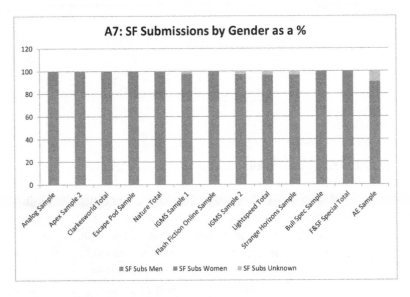

A7: SF Submissions by Gender as a %

Analog Sample, Apex Sample 2, Clarkesworld Total, Escape Pod Sample, Nature Total, IGMS Sample 1, Flash Fiction Online Sample, IGMS Sample 2, Lightspeed Total, Strange Horizons Sample, Bull Spec Sample, F&SF Special Total, AE Sample

■ SF Subs Men   ■ SF Subs Women   ■ SF Subs Unknown

No market received more submissions from women than from men.

As in the previous article, I tested to see if these differences were significant, and found:

The differences in submissions ratios between markets *are* significant, both for all submissions and science fiction submissions specifically.

Science Fiction Submissions by Genre of Market

I have no evidence to say that women make up a smaller proportion of submissions for science fiction only markets than for mixed-genre markets.

Mixed-Genre Publications: Gender Split of Total Subs vs. Gender Split of Science Fiction Subs

I found a moderate-strong positive correlation, so there is a tendency for mixed genre-publications who receive a high proportion of total submissions from one gender to also receive a high proportion of science fiction submissions from that gender.

Submissions Ratios by Gender of Senior Editorial Team

I found no significant relationships between gender of senior editorial team and gender ratios of submissions either for all stories or for science fiction stories.

Story Submission Split by Average Age of Senior Editorial Team

I found no significant relationships between age of senior editorial team and gender ratios of submissions either for all stories or for science fiction stories.

So, What Does This All Mean?

There are several interesting results from looking at the Submissions data. While there is significant variation between markets, the range is much smaller than we saw in Publications. In addition, while a significant number of markets published more women than men in the Publications data, no market received more submissions from women than from men, either overall or for science fiction. In mixed-genre markets, we see that a relatively high proportion of total submissions from one gender is correlated with a relatively high proportion of science fiction submissions from that gender.

The volume of submissions received shows dramatic variation. While these figures were estimated in some cases, it is fair to say that yearly submission volumes between markets range from a few hundred up to a few thousand. As such, the idea that gender ratios in submissions are due to the fact that women simply don't *write* science fiction is patently untrue. While this might be the case for high-volume markets, the number of science fiction stories written by women in total is far greater than the number received by many markets. For example, if approximately 30% of the science fiction submissions by women received by *Strange Horizons* were instead submitted to *Nature,* we would see an equal gender representation in *Nature's* submissions. (This is assuming that all stories submitted to *Nature* were also submitted to *Strange Horizons.* If we assume no overlap, the number is around 20%. The actual number is likely somewhere in the middle. Please note that I am aware that a suitable submissions for one market is not necessarily a good fit for another. This thought experiment serves as an illustration of the comparative volume of submissions and the effect that increased or diverted submissions from a small percentage of the women authors in the field could have on some markets.)

However, there is no obvious smoking gun which shows us *why* submissions ratios vary between markets. I found no significant correlations between gender ratios of submissions and any of the categories that we tested. Based on our data, genre of market, age of senior editorial team, and gender of senior editorial team, are not factors that are related to the ratio of submissions by men and women.

A Note on Comparing Submissions with Published Stories

This all begs the question—is there a relationship between submissions ratios and publications ratios? In the next installment, I will be looking at what further analysis can be carried out regarding this data. In the meantime, I would like to warn readers about the problems with attempting to carry out a simple analysis of the Submissions Ratios from samples, vs Publications From Slush for a whole year.

Conveniently, we have a good example of the pitfalls of this approach. Four markets provided data on the Stories Accepted from Slush during the time period of submissions data provided, which we can compare to Stories Published from Slush in the time period given in the previous article: *Clarkesworld, Bull Spec, Flash Fiction Online,* and *Lightspeed.*

Looking at the differences between what was accepted from that specific slush sample, and what was published in a full year, we can see that a simple analysis of Submissions Ratios for the samples given vs Publications from Slush for an entire year would not give an accurate picture.

Tables 6a/6b: Acceptances from Submissions Sample Time Period vs Yearly Publications

	Acceptances from Slush			
	Total	Men	Women	Non-Binary
Clarkesworld	32	11	21	0
		34.38	65.62%	0%
Bull Spec	3	2	0	1
		66.67%	0%	33.33%
Flash Fiction Online	18	8	10	0
		44.44%	55.56%	0%
Lightspeed	35	19	15	1
		54.29%	42.86%	2.86%

	Publications from Slush			
	Total	Men	Women	Non-Binary
Clarkesworld	36	11.5	24.5	0
		31.94%	68.06%	0%
Bull Spec	6	2	4	1
		33.33%	66.66%	0%
Flash Fiction Online	21	8	3	0
		38.10%	61.90%	0%
Lightspeed	48	25	23	0
		52.08%	47.92%	0%

Next Time on Adventures in Statistics: Our hero wraps things up with a pretty pink bow! Will she be able to avoid overdosing on graphs?

ABOUT THE AUTHOR

Susan E. Connolly's short fiction and non-fiction have appeared in *Strange Horizons, Daily Science Fiction, The Center For Digital Ethics* and the fanzine *Journey Planet.* She is the author of *Damsel,* a middle-grade fantasy from Mercier Press and *Granuaile,* an upcoming historical comic book from Atomic Diner. Her degree in Veterinary Medicine given her strong opinions about the accurate portrayal of animal sidekicks in fiction. Susan lives in Ireland, near the mountains. Also near the sea. Also near the forest (Ireland is a small country).

The Issue of Gender in Genre Fiction: The Math Behind the Slush

SUSAN E. CONNOLLY

Editor's Note: Knowing that some people will be curious about the math behind Susan's piece, we asked her to provide something a bit more technical for those more mathematically inclined among us.

Submissions Variation Between Markets

Hypothesis: There are no significant differences in gender ratios relationship between markets.

All Submissions
Chi Square: 248.94
Critical value at 99.9%: 34.53

I can reject the null hypothesis

Science Fiction Submissions
Chi Square: 89.6
Critical value at 99.9%: 31.26

I can reject the null hypothesis

Science Fiction Submissions by Genre of Market

Hypothesis: Science fiction only markets are not more likely to receive submissions from men.

Using a Pearson's correlation I got an R value of 0.14 (considered weak), with a T-value of 0.46 and a p value of 0.33. For a one-tailed t-test the critical value is 1.81.

Therefore I cannot reject the null hypothesis.

Non-Science Fiction-Only Publications: Gender Split of Total Subs vs. Gender Split of Science Fiction Subs

Hypothesis: There is no relationship between the gender ratio of all submissions and the gender ratio of science fiction submissions.

R value: 0.7132 (Strong positive correlation)

I can reject the null hypothesis.

All-Men Senior Editorial Team Vs All-Women or Mixed-Gender Senior Editorial Team

Hypothesis: Men-only senior editorial teams are not more likely to receive submissions from authors who are men.

All Submissions
 R value: -0.16 (weak negative correlation)
 T value: -0.57
 Critical value at 95% probability: 1.78

Based on the t-value this result is not significant.

Science Fiction Submissions
 R value: 0.23 (weak positive correlation)
 T value: 0.76
 Critical value at 95% probability: 1.81

Based on the t-value this result is not significant.

All-Women Senior Editorial Team Vs All-Men or Mixed-Gender Senior Editorial Team

Hypothesis: Women-only senior editorial teams are not more likely to receive submissions from authors who are women.

All Submissions
R value: 0.19 (weak positive correlation)
T value: 0.66
Critical value at 95% probability: 1.78

Based on the t-value this result is not significant.

Science Fiction Submissions
R value: -0.23 (weak negative correlation)
T value: 0.74
Critical value at 95% probability: 1.81

Based on the t-value this result is not significant.

Age of Senior Editorial Team

Hypothesis: Age of Senior Editorial Team Has No Relationship with the Percentage of Submissions by Authors Who Are Men

Mean Age vs. Total Subs by Men %
R value: 0.2395 (weak positive correlation)

Mean Age vs. Science Fiction Subs by Men %
R value: 0.1299 (weak positive correlation)

Median Age vs. Total Subs by Men %
R value: 0.2329 (weak positive correlation)

Median Age vs. Science Fiction Subs by Men %
R value: 0.1125 (weak positive correlation)

While the results technically show a positive correlation, the relation-ship is extremely weak, and insufficient to reject the null hypothesis.

ABOUT THE AUTHOR

Susan E. Connolly's short fiction and non-fiction have appeared in *Strange Horizons, Daily Science Fiction, The Center For Digital Ethics* and the fanzine *Journey Planet.* She is the author of *Damsel,* a middle-grade fantasy from Mercier Press and *Granuaile,* an upcoming historical comic book from Atomic Diner. Her degree in Veterinary Medicine given her strong opinions about the accurate portrayal of animal sidekicks in fiction. Susan lives in Ireland, near the mountains. Also near the sea. Also near the forest (Ireland is a small country).

Annihilation, Authority, and Acceptance: An Interview with Jeff VanderMeer

BEN FRY

Jeff VanderMeer's Southern Reach trilogy, comprised of Annihilation, Authority, and Acceptance was optioned by Paramount Pictures and foreign language rights have sold in sixteen countries. The series has been featured on the front page of the New York Times as an example of an accelerated publishing schedule, also known as "binge reading" and spotlighted by Entertainment Weekly, among many many others.

The trilogy chronicles the attempts of the secret government agency known as the Southern Reach to uncover the mystery behind Area X, a pristine wilderness existing behind an invisible border, cut off from the rest of the world for over thirty years. The first two books are already out and *Acceptance* will be published on September 2nd.

In April, VanderMeer attended the Arkansas Book Festival and participated in a Q&A with Ben Fry at the Witt Stephens Jr. Central

Arkansas Nature Center. Fry has served as General Manager of KLRE & KUAR Public Radio in Little Rock, Arkansas, since 1995. He also serves as an adjunct professor in the School of Mass Communication at the University of Arkansas at Little Rock, teaching film classes. This transcript of their conversation has been slightly abridged.

Jeff, can you talk a little bit about the beginnings of this book, how the idea came to you, and whether you were thinking of a trilogy when it first came about?

The very basic idea came to me actually in a nightmare. I was very sick with bronchitis, and one night I had this nightmare where I was walking down into a tunnel, and as I walked into the tunnel, I saw these living words written in some living material on the walls, and they were getting fresher as I went farther and farther down, which meant whatever was writing them was actually down there as well. At a certain point, I saw kind of a weird light, and I knew if I turned the corner, I would actually see whatever was down there. At that point, I think it was that my writer brain decided to airlift me out, because if I'd seen whatever was there, I wouldn't have written the story.

There were some precursors to this. I had wanted to write about the Florida Wilderness in some form for a long time, and so I had that in the back of my head. There had also been the Gulf oil spill, which at the time had been this horrible unending experience where hiking in that coastal wilderness, knowing the threat to it, and having to sit there every day not being able to do anything about it, the oil was just, and all of our heads in that area was just basically continually spilling and spilling and spilling. On some level, I think that also affected my subconscious just coming up with something like Area X to some degree, a total transformation, obviously, of the situation, but I still think that was a bit of a catalyst.

Have you always been inspired by dreams? My experience with that is I have this fantastic dream. I go, "This is a great story." I wake up, and it's absolutely ridiculous.

Yes, I have tons of dreams. I had a dream about a giant armadillo that was terrorizing Tallahassee where I live. That did not become anything, not even a story. Usually, when I have a dream, it doesn't become a story, but when characters and situations and a plot begin accrete around it, then it works. I do have a strong belief in the subconscious. There're many times working on a book where when I go to bed, I say, "Okay, subconscious, this is the problem I'm working on. I want a solution in the morning." That actually works.

Could you talk a little bit more about St. Marks, the wildlife refuge and your hikes there.

I hike out to St. Marks, which is in the [Florida] Panhandle, and there's a trail out there that's about fourteen miles, and it's a great trail to do because it goes from your standard pine forest to cypress swamp, and it goes from that to salt marsh and then from there out to the sea, and so you have all of these different environments back-to-back. It's fairly unique. You can't find a whole lot of places like that in the United States with that particular type of environment.

You see all kinds of things out there. The dolphins will come into the freshwater canals at high tide chasing fish, and they've adapted to the brackish water there, so you'll be out there hiking, and the first time I saw this, it just kind of blew my mind, because you're not expecting a dolphin. You kind of think you're in a dolphin-free zone, and suddenly you're not.

It's like the first time I was in Australia and I saw a kangaroo, a flash of brown come out of the underbrush, it's the same thing because I was used to flashes of brown meaning a deer. You see things like that that are natural to the area, but they seem really strange if you don't live there and experience them a few times.

So sometimes I get reactions to the books where people are reacting to things that actually happened in the wilderness, but they're not accustomed to that area of the wilderness, or they don't go hiking a lot, and so the books are even stranger for them than they are for other people.

I did actually once thought I saw a kangaroo out [at St. Marks, too] which I know couldn't have been a kangaroo, but I was with someone who was saying, "Look, there's an alligator over there," and so I saw this "kangaroo" out of the corner of my eye, turned to look at the alligator, and [when I tried to find the kangaroo again], it wasn't there anymore. I'll never know what it was.

I did encounter a Florida panther out there. It's an unconfirmed sighting because I was there by myself, and I didn't take a picture, but there are no other cats that large with tails in Florida. That was something.

Is that an important part of writing these novels, the environment? Is that important to you, natural settings?

Yeah, it really is. This is just the first time I've really had an opportunity to engage at length with it to some degree. Before, most of my novels have been set in cities, so it's been obviously a more urban environment. It's been really kind of satisfying to really write about the place that's closest to my heart, that I really feel is home.

When I was a child, we traveled around so much I didn't really have a place that I could write about, like Stephen King writes about Maine. After close to twenty years hiking at St. Marks, I really feel close to it, and I feel comfortable with it. That's one reason why I could write the novel so quickly: the whole landscape is basically the fourteen-mile hike, including the lighthouse.

In fact, when I finished it, I handed it to my wife, and I said, "I think I just wrote something incomprehensible about four women wandering aimlessly on a hiking trail in North Florida. Could you please check for me?" She read it and thankfully gave it the stamp of approval and said it was actually a novel and actually made sense.

Then in *Authority,* which is set in kind of like small towns in part and the secret agency, it gave me an opportunity to show wildlife kind of interacting in that context and the way that we, even in small towns and whatnot, we encounter animals. A slightly more urban setting. We still are interacting with our environment in an interesting way.

When I was reading Annihilation, there was this point where I really felt like I couldn't trust anything that anybody said, including the narrator . . . I even started to wonder whether what she was telling me was happening was authentic or not. Is that intentional?

Yeah, it is intentional that this novel destabilizes you section by section. You think you're reading one kind of novel. Then you think you're reading another kind of novel. Then you just slowly kind of descend into this world where you're having to yourself analyze what's going on and say, "Is this accurate? Is this not accurate?" You kind of descend into the paranoia because you get a sense, I think, pretty early on, so it's not a spoiler, that the agency that's sending them in is pretty paranoid itself and hasn't told them everything like the excerpt that I read.

You have that. Then you have whatever is in Area X being a really good mimic and at times throwing back things at you that it thinks you want to see. If the biologist is inaccurate, it's because she's being misled. I think she's not so much an unreliable narrator as somebody who doesn't want to tell you everything at the time you want to hear it. Everything she says is accurate up to a point. It's just that she's not telling everything.

Especially in the third book, you learn a lot more about her too and get a better sense of maybe peculiarities of her character you don't know about in book one, and also by book three, a lot of the conversations that occur in *Annihilation* take on a different light because you know a lot more about those other characters on the expedition with her, because some of the other two books go back into the past a little bit.

There's a style in it too that I think you do which is the characters hold back information. In Authority, I noticed that sometimes I would think that there would be an incident that will happen, and I will think it's all over with, and then a few pages later, you come back, and you hear there was something really important that happened in that incident that wasn't explained at that time. What's your intention with that?

[In part because the main character is trying to analyze everything and put it into a context first, and also because the point at which some things happen to the main character isn't the point of maximum tension—it's when he has to report back to his superiors. But] there's also a real practical reason why [for some of] those gaps, so I can't really address that. With the biologist, she's very concerned about being seen as objective and not being judged by certain things, so her agenda when she sets out this journal account, which is written . . . it's not really in the moment of what's happening but a little bit afterwards . . . she's very concerned about that, and so there's certain things she doesn't want to let you know, because she wants you to have other information first. I also think she's kind of a reticent person anyway, somebody who kind of interacts with the wilderness a lot more than she does with other people or has more of an affinity for so . . .

The first novel's first person, the second novel is third person. Did you think at some point about writing the second novel in first person?

No, I pretty much always knew the second novel was going to be third person. It was from the point of view of a new director taking over the Southern Reach, the secret agency, and I always knew that it was better for me to do that in third person.

Somehow, my way into his character was third person, not first person, maybe because I think that if you're new coming into the situation, you can already feel a little overwhelmed, and being so close as first person to that character probably would've meant it would be very difficult to get a sense of what's going on around him, and so I wanted a little bit of separation from him, even though I'm very interior on his thoughts, to be able to kind of show the wider view of things.

In the third book, I use first, second, and third for different character points of view. Something that really annoys me with multiple character novels is when they use all first person. It's really hard to make those differentiated, and if you use too many third person points of view, then the same problem can occur, just not as giant. Using the mix of the three makes them really stand out from one another, because the second person one is set in the past.

Did they get progressively longer. Is Acceptance a lot longer than Authority?

The second one is ninety-three thousand words, and the third one is about ninety-one thousand. Almost twice [the length of Annihilation], and they're all very complete, separate novels. There's parts of the third one you probably can't read without reading the first two, but the first two you can read independent of one another. You could conceivable read Authority first and then read Annihilation. It would be a different reading experience, but the reveals and the mysteries are so different in what's happening that you wouldn't have any spoilers, one from the other really.

I think Annihilation works all alone too. You don't necessary have to know all the things that you're going to find out in the next novels.

That's correct, and that's why they're not this A to B to C bunch of reveals because it's actually been really rewarding to me, because I like ambiguity quite a bit, to have a certain number of readers saying, "I don't even want to know what happens next. There's enough in this for me." Then, of course, there're readers who say, "I need to know what these mysteries." I think I struck a balance between those two groups. It'll be probably enough for them to both hate me by the end of the series. [Laughing]

Seriously, *Authority* is an exploration of authority as well as a continuation of the story. It is its own separate character arc. It is about this secret agency. It's an expedition into it the same way that *Annihilation*'s an expedition into Area X, and then the third book has its own set of themes and concerns.

Reveals are like ten to twenty sentences a book, and then there's all the rest of it [remaining to write]. Conceivably, I could've written book one and done a couple Twitter messages and been done, I suppose, but there were some other things I wanted to explore, and I really wanted to explore these characters from different points of view. Even by the end of the second book, you have a different view of the psychologist, who's on the expedition in the first book, for example.

The publishing experience was different for you from what you have been used to. Would you talk a little bit about that?

Yeah, it was quite interesting. Up until this point, I'd been writing books that were set in imaginary worlds. They were published by science fiction fantasy publishers here in the US. Sometimes they were published by mainstream publishers overseas. On this one, it was the exact reverse. We had several offers from literary mainstream imprints and very little interest from genre imprints, and I still don't know why that was. I was kind of concerned until the books came out, and does this mean it's not going to connect with a certain segment of readers?

But so far, these are probably my best-selling books ever. I think the schedule that they're on of releasing all three in the same year has been really helpful too in terms of sometimes you'll have the second book come out a year later, and even if people really loved the first book, there's this resistance to it, or they have forgotten certain parts, and so there was also less need for me to kind of recap things at the beginning of the second book that there would've been otherwise.

The only thing about the fact that they're putting them out back to back is I think I'm probably going to be dead by the end because I've been on the road more or less continuously except for some breaks from February 4th through now, and then I get two months off, and then I go back on the road from the end of June to the end of the year.

I get a year off after this, and after living like a hermit for two years, I get to be on the road and learn how to talk to people again, which has been fascinating as well.

Which one do you like better, the hermit or road warrior.

The hermit because I love to write, but I do love being out on the road. Now, I schedule some extra time to go walking around the wilderness. I enjoy meeting people, but every once in a while, at a certain point I have to kind of retreat and get some writing time in. There's kind of an itch there where if I don't write for a very long time, I get kind of twitchy. Luckily you're not encountering me when I'm twitchy.

Audience: What about you doing the screenplay for the movie?

That's a very good question. Because it's a first person narrative and film is third person, they're going to have to make radical changes anyway to make the first movie, so I don't really have a problem with someone else doing the screenplay. If it was somebody other than Scott Rudin Productions, maybe I would have a problem.

Well, thinking about the film, are there things that you are concerned about?

I'm concerned about a few things. These are not four white women running round in Annihilation, as you learn in the second book. They're also not a bunch of men, and my concern would be that they would change the gender of the characters or something like that. I'm less concerned on the diversity issue because it's more about getting the right actor. [Regina King] who was on Southland who I think would be perfect to play the biologist, even though you learn the biologist is not African-American in the second book. It's more getting the mix right, getting the right actresses, sticking with women for that expedition. Those would be my main concerns would be casting concerns.

In fact, that's what I was thinking about. I would hate to see them change the female expedition because we've got to have a guy in there. There's a tendency to do that with a science fiction thriller, to not have it all be led by women. That concerned me too.

I read somewhere recently that a lot of the top blockbusters have had female leads, so maybe that's changing.

Your parents, growing up in Fiji, what kind of influences has that had on your writing over the years?

There's a scene in Annihilation where she goes out at night, and she finds this glowing starfish. This is actually something that happened to me when I was in Fiji at like the age of six or seven. We were out on the reef at night, and . . . at a certain point I had no idea where the heck I was and which way land was or anything else. I could kind of see flashlights in the distance, and I came across this Crown-of-Thorns starfish, which does kind of have a phosphorescence at night. It kind of acclimated me to exactly where I was.

Other than that, I haven't been able to write about Fiji, and I don't know if it's because I was so young when I was there or because being embedded in another culture doesn't really mean you become an expert on where you are. Definitely, it was an influence because instead of taking raises or sometimes pay, what they did is they took travel vouchers and at the age of, I think, I was eight or nine when we came back from the Peace Corps from Fiji, we spent nine months traveling around the world, mostly Southeast Asia and Africa and places like that, and it was the perfect age for me to soak up a lot of it and, of course, have an influence on my fiction and how I think about fiction in general.

Your parents, I think, somewhat show up in the books.

They do a little bit. They're kind of transformed. They appeared a little bit more in my prior novels. My dad's an ant scientist. He's a research chemist with the USDA working on fire ants. My mom's a biological illustrator and currently studying French graveyard art for another Ph.D. over in France. In fact, she once got caught in a graveyard after hours and was detained by the police and then emailed me and said, "You wouldn't believe how many weird people there are in this graveyard after midnight." I was like, "Yes, mom, you were there."

How important is research in your writing? In this particular, in the first book, Annihilation, you've got a biologist and a psychiatrist. You've got all these scientists. How important is it for you to kind of know where they're coming from?

Even though my dad's an "ant scientist," he has interaction with other kinds of scientists, and there are certain things that are common across in terms of scientific theory and pursuit. That I already kind of had down, and then I did do some research. I always wanted to be a marine biologist until I discovered I didn't really want to study biology—I just wanted to look in tidal pools—and so I had some background there.

I also had the idea that the biologist is not the world's best biologist. I mean, you notice in the book that she gets fired from an awful lot of jobs. I used that in part because I didn't want to over-research it and then kill the spontaneity of the book with too much of that. There're actions that she takes that are not really by the book that wind up being important to the plot in the second and the third book.

You know, you also write things that kind of take place in imaginary cities and involve history. Do you spend a lot of time researching that sort of thing?

For the prior books, I studied pretty much all of Byzantine history. I must have read twenty to thirty books on Byzantine history and Venetian history. There're some really weird things in there—like you find out that the Visigoths made cloaks from the pelts of field mice and that the leaders who had the most power had the most field mouse pelts in their cloaks. That sounds very powerful. [Laughter]

For the Southern Reach novels, it was more the sense of place that was really important, and so I reached this point in writing where I knew I needed to have a different environment because at some point one of the characters leaves the South basically, and I was a little bit frantic about that because everything in the books that's about the South is something that I've seen, observed, know the texture of, and I didn't want a single received research detail in there.

So my wife and I actually took two weeks off to just go up the coast of California as basically a research trip, and what I was doing was collecting textures and smells and scents and talking to people. You can't feel like you live there obviously if you've only been there for that amount of time, but in terms of the actual landscape, you can pick up enough detail, enough sense of it, that you're not giving reader received secondhand information.

Audience: What did you study in college?

Well, I went to the University of Florida, and I took some creative writing classes. I started out as a journalism major and then went to English with a Latin American History minor, and then by the second year I pretty much I knew I didn't really feel like graduating. I know that sounds weird, so I just took every class I wanted to take that I hadn't taken because the poet Richard Wilbur had come through a couple of years before, and he basically said don't get a creative writing degree—just take as many different courses as possible. Learn as much as possible, soak everything in.

At that point, I just had lost focus because I didn't want to become a teacher or journalist. I just wanted to write fiction. I dropped out halfway through my senior year, and I got a tech writing job, and then I just wrote on the side until I could become a full-time writer. I wouldn't necessarily advise that as a path. It's just what happened to me. It's very difficult when you go in thinking you want to do one thing and then you realize it doesn't really matter what you do because all you want to do is write fiction. That's very destabilizing when you're in a situation where you need to have discipline.

Audience: Do you have a good idea about the characters' names and who they are and where they are? Since there are no names in* Annihilation *and you don't know exactly where in the world it's set.

In Authority, you get a better idea of most of them. You get some names. You may never get a name for the biologist; I'm not telling. And you get more of a sense of place, very specific. Like, the Southern Reach building in Authority is based on a combination of really crappy 1970s concrete government buildings in the United States and like the worst possible Soviet architectural disasters, so it's this kind of U that has all these weird baffle issues and all these gutter issues. I had a lot of fun with that where actually, for the second novel, I have a diagram of the building and how everything matches up.

We mentioned that the story has a kind of espionage thing going on. What was your inspiration for that?

I'm a huge John Le Carre fan. I think he is a brilliant writer, and for some reason—and this doesn't lessen the accomplishment—in his best novels, I think he's just an absolutely master of the art and craft of writing, but because they're espionage novels and therefore they have this particular focus, it's easier to see how he uses craft than in some mainstream literary novels that are not in a particular genre. Even though, like I said, I think he's absolutely a master of that.

I love the interiority of some of his characters, the way that he makes all his characters incredible lived-in, and you just see everything from their perspective in such an interesting way and how they get involved in these very intricate puzzles. I've taken a lot of craft lessons from reading Le Carre's books, and I wanted to do kind of a deconstructed spy story mixed with kind of a horror story.

You've mentioned your wife a couple of times. I know you edit anthologies together. What's the working relationship like.

It didn't start out very well. We met because she came down to Gainesville where I was organizing some literary events, and she was asking for advice about her magazine, which she just started. I promptly then sent her a story. This was very early in my career. It was a terrible story about a talking magic frog going to the prom, and I don't even . . . I mean, it was really, really early in my career.

She rejected it, and then I sent her a letter back saying that I was glad she rejected it. It had been a test to see if she was a good editor. [Laughter] Which it had not been. It was just a crappy story that I had not recognized was a crappy story. Our relationship built on that. As most relationships do.

For a long time, we kept our editing separate because we wanted to have separate identities, and we were both afraid, just because of sexism in the field, that if we combined forces everything would be about me. Then eventually, it made no sense because she was helping on all the projects I was doing, and I was helping on all the projects she was doing, so we combined forces, and now we've edited all these anthologies together, and it's proven very good.

I'm a good skimmer if that makes any sense, on these anthologies. I will go on ahead like a golden retriever bringing back interesting stuff, and she will tell me, "That wasn't actually very interesting at all," or "This was." She's the more in-depth reader for the anthology. She's also a very good general editor, and I'm more about the line edits and getting into the manuscript, and so we work very well in that regard.

After the third novel comes out and you've finished your travels where do you go from there? I know you're not going to think about writing fiction for a year, right?

Right. Well, I'm working on editing for our own press an omnibus of a really interesting Finnish writer, Leena Krohn, a nine hundred-page volume of her work. I think she's an amazing fantasy writer who's very underappreciated, and my hope is that when all of these reviewers get this doorstop of a book, there's absolutely no way that they can ignore her work.

I'm also working on something called *The Book Murderer*, which I meant to be the last novel I ever wrote but probably will be the next one, which is a sendup of all aspects of book culture. From publishing to reviewers to everything, every aspect of it, literary festivals. This festival nothing weird has happened, so I have no material.

Well, yeah, it's not over yet.

Ha! Yes, and, you know, the book addresses issues like blurbing. Blurbing can be a very kind of incestuous thing where you blurb somebody, and then they ask you for a blurb, and so there's a section in The Book Murderer where he does a rant on his blog about blurbers, and the whole incestuous nature is completely over the top. The reason I know this might get me in trouble is I posted on my blog just as an experiment to see how people would react, and I got so much hate mail from this thing that was meant to be a parody or a satire.

Thank you very much.

Thank you. Thank you for some great questions.

ABOUT THE AUTHOR

Ben Fry is the General Manager of UALR Public Radio.

Another Word:
Reclaiming the Tie-In Novel
JAMES L. SUTTER

Our society has a weird relationship with logos. Put a popular brand name on a t-shirt, and you'll find people happy to pay fifty dollars (or two hundred dollars for Gucci!) to be a walking billboard. But put the logo of a popular game or film property on a novel cover, and suddenly genre readers will be falling all over themselves to tell you how they love fantasy and science fiction, but they don't read those novels.

What's even stranger is that it's not even true. Look at the bestseller lists, and you'll find Star Wars, Halo, and Dungeons & Dragons right up there with George R. R. Martin and Brandon Sanderson. There's a reason you recognize names like Margaret Weis, R. A. Salvatore, and Ed Greenwood, and it's that books based on popular properties *sell*.

They also inspire. After most of a decade working in the fantasy and gaming fields, I've yet to meet an author under fifty who, when questioned, didn't admit to being inspired by tie-in novels at some point. We all read Dragonlance. We all fervently wished for George Lucas to make Timothy Zahn's Thrawn Trilogy instead of the blasphemous prequels. We all know what kind of swords Drizzt uses (twin scimitars).

So why do so many of us now turn up our noses at such things?

The easy answer is that a lot of tie-in is bad—literary pap churned out by authors and editors who don't care about quality as long as the machine keeps turning. But like most easy answers, that's a bit disingenuous. As Theodore Sturgeon taught us, 90% of *everything* is crap, and I've certainly read plenty of creator-owned fantasy that might fit that description as well. So why do we place tie-in on a lower rung in the artistic hierarchy?

You'll notice that I keep saying "we." This isn't just a literary device. For many years, I held the same opinion. As a kid, I devoured tie-in for everything from Dungeons & Dragons to Star Wars to Indiana Jones. Yet when I hit my punk-rock teens, I started questioning my former infatuation. The fact that tie-in required an author to work with an IP holder—a *corporation*—no longer jived with my concept of art. Surely *real* artists wouldn't allow themselves to be impacted by the forces of commerce. These authors of "corporate fiction," as I called it, must be sellouts and has-beens.

That opinion lasted right up until I started working in publishing, at which point I discovered that my entire concept of how books were made was hopelessly naïve. Authors—even of creator-owned works—rarely operate in a vacuum. The idea of a novel as a pure and perfect transmission from author to reader tends to shatter the first time an author gets revision notes back from an editor. And as for being free from the forces of capitalism—well, *maybe* in self-publishing, but last I checked most publishers are in the business of making money, and an author who doesn't work with them to try and maximize sales tends not to be their author for long.

But the final nail in the coffin of my anti-tie-in prejudice was provided by the authors themselves. You see, there were simply too many good authors doing it. And not just good authors within the tie-in world—big name authors that had won awards and published bestsellers doing creator-owned work kept turning up in the mix. Brandon Sanderson. Greg Bear. Tobias Buckell. If you really want your head to spin, wrap your brain around the fact that Nicola Griffith—perhaps the leading voice in feminist and queer SF, with enough major awards to deck out a Christmas tree—wrote stories for *Warhammer* back in the 80s!

These authors didn't suddenly lose their chops just because they were writing tie-in. If an awesome author can write tie-in, then it must follow that *tie-in can be awesome.*

This realization came none too soon for me, as it was around this time that I was put in charge of launching Pathfinder Tales, a line of novels set in the world of the Pathfinder Roleplaying Game. As the Managing Editor for Paizo Publishing, I've been on a mission ever since to help tear down the idea that tie-in fiction is somehow inherently lesser than creator-owned fiction. Toward that end, I've made it my mission to not just hire from inside established tie-in author circles, but to reach out to mainstream fantasy and science fiction authors as well. Along with popular tie-in authors like Ed Greenwood and Elaine Cunningham,

I've also been fortunate enough to bring in authors like Hugo Award-winner Tim Pratt, Howard Andrew Jones, and Liane Merciel.

While tie-in work obviously isn't for everyone, as the representative of The Establishment, I see it as my duty to give authors as much creative control and ownership as possible over their characters and plots. We provide the world, they provide the stories.

As a writer, tie-in work is an admittedly mixed bag. I've personally written two Pathfinder novels, *Death's Heretic* and *The Redemption Engine,* and while *Death's Heretic* ending up at #3 on Barnes & Noble's Best Fantasy Releases of 2011 did a fair bit to quiet naysayers (especially the ones inside my own head), there were plenty of friends who cautioned me against getting into tie-in. As one longtime editor put it, I ran the risk of getting "stuck in the tie-in ghetto." Certainly tie-in doesn't often win awards. And unlike a creator-owned project, if you *do* get a hit, you don't own the rights to your work, and that money goes primarily into the IP-holder's pocket.

Yet as one of my authors, Dave Gross, once said: "In tie-in, the ceiling may be lower, but the floor is higher." It's true that if your tie-in character gets huge and ends up on happy meals and Saturday morning cartoons, you're not going to see much of that money. At the same time, however, tie-in comes with a built-in audience. Especially for new authors, there's always the chance that a creator-owned novel will stall out at a few hundred copies (or, god forbid, a few dozen). In tie-in, however, a lot of that risk is ameliorated. You can release your new novel knowing that there are thousands of fans of the brand who'll buy that book *even if they have no idea who you are.* And while it's no guarantee, the hope is that some of these fans will then go out and buy your creator-owned work.

There's another huge incentive for tie-in writers as well, and that's the nature of tie-in itself. When you see somebody like Greg Bear writing for Star Wars, do you really think it's just about the money? Or do you think it's because, like the rest of us, he's spent a lifetime enjoying that universe, and is eager to play with the toys? At its root, tie-in is fan fiction that you get paid for, and gives you the chance to say to your friends, "You know that thing we love? Well I'm now *officially* a part of it." As an editor and game designer, some of my favorite moments come when authors I respect contact me to let me know that they're playing Pathfinder at home.

And as much as working within an established world can tie your hands, it can also prop you up. I've had several authors tell me that they love writing tie-in because it allows them to outsource the part of

SF writing they're shakiest on—the world-building—and focus more energy on plot and character. While I'm admittedly a world-builder first and foremost—hence my day job—even I have to admit that it's a thrill to be able to cherry-pick the best ideas from a team of incredible world-builders and incorporate them into my own work.

As a young punk, I rebelled against tie-in as evidence of The Man holding artists down. Now, as an older and (hopefully) wiser punk, I want us to rebel against what's really holding us down: bullshit hierarchies. As self-avowed nerds, we ought to know the unfairness of being arbitrarily placed on a low social rung. We rail against mainstream society not understanding us, and bemoan those backward literary critics who disparage science fiction and fantasy as "wish fulfillment for young boys." Yet we then turn around and build our own elaborate hierarchies to put each other down. Video gamers look down on roleplayers who look down on LARPers who insist that at least they're not *furries*.

All of which is simply spitting on others so that we can ignore the spit on our own heads. That's third-grade playground politics. In this era where we've got supercomputers in our pockets and robots trundling around Mars, is that really the best we can do?

Perhaps my tone is too strident for a conversation about tie-in fiction. There are plenty of causes more worthy of impassioned speeches (and I fully expect this space will be used for them, by authors far more qualified to speak than I am). Yet whether our biases are big or small, artistic or social, questioning them is how we move forward and grow as people, as a subculture, and as a society.

So let's stop judging books by their covers.

ABOUT THE AUTHOR

James L. Sutter is the Managing Editor for Paizo Publishing and a co-creator of the Pathfinder Roleplaying Game. He is the author of the novels *Death's Heretic* and *The Redemption Engine,* the former of which was #3 on Barnes & Noble's list of the Best Fantasy Releases of 2011 and a finalist for the Compton Crook Award for Best First Novel and an Origins Award. He's written short stories for such publications as *Escape Pod, Apex Magazine, Beneath Ceaseless Skies, Geek Love,* and the #1 Amazon bestseller *Machine of Death.* His anthology *Before They Were Giants* pairs the first published short stories of science fiction luminaries with new interviews and writing advice from the authors themselves. In addition, he's published a wealth of gaming material for both Dungeons & Dragons and the Pathfinder Roleplaying Game.

Editor's Desk:
Adding Some Color
NEIL CLARKE

When something nearly kills you, it's hard to avoid thinking about it. These events worm their way into your mind and color almost everything. Two years since my heart attack, my doctors continue to remind me that I'm very lucky to be alive.

Every morning, the voice in my head makes sure to echo that sentiment. Every morning, I push back the darkness and try to be the good little survivor. It's not easy, but I have a loving family, good friends, and this job to help bolster me. I won't lie. Some days it beats me up. Some worse than others.

The anniversary of that event likes to taunt me. Last year I fought back against the blues by scheduling the end of my cyborg anthology Kickstarter campaign to conclude on the first anniversary of the heart attack. The reponse to *UPGRADED* exceeded initial funding goals and the experience allowed me to color that date my own way. I continue to be grateful to everyone that participated. I enjoyed working on this project and learned a lot in the process. More good news: that project is finally done and copies will start shipping to supporters later this month.

I had hoped that by this second anniversary, I'd be well on my way in making *Clarkesworld* my full time job as my current employment is a constant source of stress. Shortly after my heart attack, I wrote in one of my editorials:

"To my knowledge, there hasn't been an independent online magazine that has successfully made the jump to paying authors and staff professional rates without dipping into the publisher's pockets or becoming a patron of some other organization. This doesn't mean it can't be done." We've made progress, but still have a long way to go.

I've always acknowledged that for us to reach that big goal, *Clarkesworld* had to expand. To that end, we promised to add extra stories to each issue when monthly subscriber and Patreon (patreon.com/clarkesworld) goals had been reached. In June, we reached the first of three Patreon goals!

Starting in August, we will have four original stories in every other issue. If we receive an additional $250 per issue in Patreon pledges by the end of August, there will be four stories in three of every four issues. At $500, it's four in every issue.

So it looks like I have something new to color this month with after all. And that doesn't even take into consideration some of the secret projects that are still bubbling behind-the-scenes. This could shape up to be a *very* interesting year.

ABOUT THE AUTHOR

Neil Clarke is the editor of *Clarkesworld Magazine,* owner of Wyrm Publishing and a current Hugo Award Nominee for Best Editor (short form). He currently lives in NJ with his wife and two children.

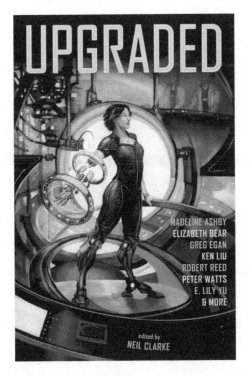

About the Artist

ALBERT URMANOV

Albert Urmanov is a twenty-five year old artist from Anshero-Sudshensk, Russia. His passion for art manifested in school, where he would draw superhero fanart for his classmates. He later went on to become a designer for several media agencies and a freelance artist before landing his current job, an internship as a concept artist at Goodgame Studios in Hamburg. Aside from creating art, he enjoys akido, anime, and hanging out with his wife and friends.

WEBSITE

albyu.cghub.com

CPSIA information can be obtained
at www.ICGtesting.com
Printed in the USA
FSHW011250250920
74138FS